Banff, the Wild Side

Daniel Hance Page

PTP
PTP Book Division
Path to Publication Group, Inc.
Arizona

Copyright © 2021 Daniel Hance Page
Printed in the United States of America
All Rights Reserved

This is a work of fiction. Any names or characters, businesses or places, events or incidents, are fictitious. Any resemblance to actual persons, living or dead, or actual events is purely coincidental. No part of this book may be used or reproduced by any means, graphic, electronic, or mechanical, including photocopying, recording, taping or by any information storage retrieval system without the written permission of the publisher except in the case of brief quotations embodied in articles and reviews.

Reviewers may quote passages for use in periodicals, newspapers, or broadcasts provided credit is given to *Banff, the Wild Side* by Daniel Hance Page and PTP Book Division, Path to Publication Group, Inc.

PTP Book Division
Path to Publication Group, Inc.
16845 E. Avenue of the Fountains, Ste.325
Fountain Hills, AZ 85268
www.ptpbookdivision.com

ISBN: 9798728489153
Library of Congress Cataloging Number
LCCN: 2021937434
Printed in the United States of America
First Edition

Dedication

Marg, Hank, Jim, Ivadelle, Sheldon, Colleen, Shane, Shannon Page, John, Dan and the Robinson family, Lester and Rose Anderson, Doug, Don, Bob Sephton and families, Garry and the Pratt family, the Massey family, Murray, Sue and the Shearer family, Joe and Linda Hill, Macari Bishara, Joan LeBoeuf, Kevin, Alison and Michaela Griffin, Jerry and Gay McFarland, Dr. David and June Chambers, "Mac" McCormick, Grant Saunders, Frank Lewis and other friends with whom we have enjoyed the wilderness

Left to right: Jim Page (Writer's brother), John Robinson (Friend), Dan Robinson (John's son), Dan Page (Writer)

Other books by Daniel Hance Page

Florida Journeys
Wilderness Journeys
Pelican Sea, a legend of Florida
Walk Upon the Clouds, a Legend of The Rocky Mountains
The Pirate and the Gunfighter
The First Americans and Their Achievements
Life is a Fishing Trip
Riley, the Dog Visitor
Bear Trap Mountain
Where Wilderness Lives
Many Winters Past
The Journey of Jeremiah Hawken
Told By the Ravens
The Maui Traveler
Wilderness Trace
Arrowmaker
Trail of the River
Pelican Moon
Legend of the Uintas

"In God's Wilderness Lies the Hope of the World—the Great, the Fresh Unblighted Wilderness."

John Muir

Chapter 1

Gray Hawk

1870

Gray Hawk was a respected Kootenay leader who could look beyond what others could see and behold the future. He was aware of the spiritual world that seemed to take him away often. After sitting on a ledge overlooking the Bow River in the valley of what would become Banff National Park, he would return to his village with a faraway look in his gray eyes as if in spirit he had not yet returned.

This morning, however, while dawn was breaking, he was not on a ledge walking with spirits following the path of an eagle or great bear. Today, he was leading many others in defense of the winter's food supply. Buffalo meat had been packed on horses being led along a mountain trail back to the Kootenay village. This supply of food was being attacked by a large number of Sioux rapidly approaching the far side of the next hill and not all the Kootenay were trying to escape. Others, led by Gray Hawk, swept over the top of the hill and slammed into the Sioux with such fury a Sioux horse was knocked backwards into a cloud of dust where hooves flashed and the rider was crushed. Other Sioux also fell, hit so unexpectedly by club, arrow or spear.

Gray Hawk signaled a retreat and the Kootenay vanished over the top of the hill. They regrouped and attacked, catching the enemies by surprise a second time, sending more of them tumbling into rising dust. Their leader also fell, his power broken and the others scattered.

Reassembling, the Kootenay were in awe of their leader who had brought them another great victory. He had known the cold winds of many winters and each one had put a line on his face leaving it as patterned as the prairie. His features were strong and eyes gray, long ago giving a name to this person who in his spirit could fly with the hawk. The sight of a bloodied arrowhead protruding below Gray Hawk's shoulder tempered elation over such a victory.

"I'll help you, as would any of the others," proclaimed Standing Bear, a man who seemed to be all muscle and now rode next to Gray Hawk.

"Thank you," replied the older man. "You have always been a trusted friend. I can look after this wound. I can no longer protect our winter food. You can do this. I will meet you back at our village where our people wait for us."

"As you say," replied the man before he turned his horse and started riding away with the others.

My friends are leaving, thought Gray Hawk—*and so maybe is my life. From the rush of battle, I'm now stirred by joy of victory. I've led my friends to a sharp defeat of our enemies. We have acquired and protected our supply of buffalo meat. I have a package of food and I will seek shelter to heal my wound. I know I could not keep up with the others. If I slowed their progress the supplies would be endangered. My friends understand that also but would not leave me so I had to ask to be left behind. They agree such a decision is sensible because I am a healer and know the remedies.*

After moving down mountain slopes, sunlight is presently sweeping across grass on these hills and should be bringing me warmth I do not feel, observed Gray Hawk. *Sun's brightness I also do not see. The day for me has become cool and gray because I know I am probably dying.*

Stirring his horse to a quicker pace, Gray Hawk came to a mountain trail bordered by a wide, shallow, fast-flowing stream. The pony stopped and looked at the water. Gray Hawk stepped off his back, answering the request made for water. They both walked to the river and drank before wading farther. The horse started to roll in the stream. While hooves raked the sky, smooth pebbles massaged tired muscles. Gray Hawk also rested his back against pebbles, letting frigid water stir away thoughts of life ending.

With the plunge over, horse and companion rider continued the journey. *There is so much to the world that people don't see, especially when they treat living creatures as just objects*, reflected Gray Hawk who always traveled further by thought than by country. *My horse is not just transportation. He is a friend and we communicate. The pony stopped and looked at the stream, telling me he would like to go for a roll. By working with him, my life was also enhanced. Everything communicates if people would only watch and listen. All aspects are part of this life—not just people. I know I can I sleep on the trail and my horse will bring me to my lodge. Presently he's taking the route to the cave. I will go there for my healing and likely to die although I know nothing dies. I will just return to the spirit world. From there all of us have come and will return when our chosen number of years have been completed. I have heard friends say they would do their lives over again just as they were but I would not. I don't want to repeat any of my mistakes. The chance of me surviving this wound is slim and survival, if it happens, will take much time.*

I can't bring my horse into the cave and too many dangers lurk outside for him to survive being left alone by the entrance. The pony has often taken me home when I was asleep. I'll tell him to continue back to the village by saying the word, "home". At the cave's entrance, Gray Hawk rubbed the pony's sides with bunched grass before repeating the word, "home", and this companion started walking along a route leading back to the village.

Gray Hawk collected medicine plants and prepared an ointment before entering the cave. Its entrance was concealed by brush. *My guide and totem, the great bear, showed me this cave that has been used by the ancient ones*, he recalled. *When I was young, starting out on my vision quest, the first of many, I watched as this hidden place was disclosed by the great bear where its outline was placed on an interior wall. I have added a mark of a paw on the top of each of my hands.*

Inside the rock-walled room, air was scented by the medicine of a warm pool. Its surface was stirred by hot water flowing through breaks in rocks. On a smooth section of one wall, there was etched a form of a bear. Adjacent to it, there were outlines of paws.

Sufficient light came from the entrance to brighten the interior where on the floor there were charred remnants of past fires.

Having placed his possessions including a package of meat at the back of the room, Gray Hawk went outside to collect additional supplies. He gathered more healing plants before cutting firewood along with skewers and boughs.

Returning to the chamber, he wove boughs together to form a bed then skewered a piece of meat. With preparations completed, he removed the broken and bloodied shaft that had been protruding from below his shoulder. To this wound, he immediately applied ointment he had prepared. Lastly, he drank some of the pool's healing water before wading deeper and floating, letting soothing warmth bring comfort to what had become constant pain to the upper part of his body.

He rested for the first time since leaving his lodge in the village beside a river surrounded by lofty walls of mountains. Suddenly he missed home and knew his horse would soon be returning. His life again was separated from the others. This time was different, however, because with his ability to see further than most, he knew he likely could not return.

He left the water, stretched out on the bed of boughs and soon drifted into a feverish sleep. Occasionally he stirred and went outside to relieve himself before succumbing again to sleep. Aware of days passing, he sometimes kindled a fire to roast buffalo meat on a skewer. Having been nourished by this tender food and sipping water from the pond, he returned to sleep.

Always he seemed to be floating, both when he was on the water or in dreams. This sensation continued until he heard tapping sounds of a person approaching the cave.

Most light was blocked from the chamber as the form of a person filled the entrance. Just as quickly, the intruder stepped aside, letting light return and Gray Hawk exclaimed, "Raven."

"Grandfather," shouted the woman.

He remembered as much as saw her long black hair surrounding delicate yet strong facial features with flashing, dark eyes. Her smile brightened the shadows.

"I knew you'd be at your cave—your favorite place," she explained after sitting down. "When your horse returned, I followed his tracks. As I suspected all along, you are again where we have visited many times before. You have taught me the healing powers of plants. Now your knowledge is going to help you."

"Like me, you are a healer," he replied. "You have the sight also. You can see further than others."

"You have trained me well," she affirmed.

"Some things can't be taught—they are gifts," observed Gray Hawk.

"I must first work on your wound," she stated before bringing a leather bag forward to remove medications. "This drink will lessen the fever," she added while pouring liquid from a pouch to a wooden cup.

Having received the ointments, Gray Hawk drank the liquid. Afterward, he said, "A good taste to your medicine."

"You had already applied ointment to your wound," she noted.

"Yes," he replied. "Mainly I've been sleeping. I have walked in the spirit world to visit in advance the home we all left and to it we will return."

"I came here to delay your return," she declared.

"Kind of you to try," he said before Raven stepped out of the cave, coming back quickly with additional firewood. She rebuilt the fire then over it skewered two trout she had caught while traveling to the cave.

When the meat was cooked both people dined quietly on the richly scented, moist fish. Raven prepared tea and served it then they both relaxed while sipping the soothing drink.

Flames sending shadows dancing across rock walls provided a backdrop to Gray Hawk's voice as it filled the cave and returned to Raven memories of her grandfather's wondrous legends. "While we live we learn," he said, commencing a story of years since the time when the great bear's outline was carved upon the wall. Spirits of the past seemed to be present as the far-seeing two people joined again a song of words and the wondrous stories they told.

"In the beginning of the movement of people on this land," resumed the voice, "those who spoke the Algonkian language, largely the Ojibway, came from the borders of salt water in the east. Likely because of Iroquoian speaking people pushing from the south, the Algonkians continued westward, moving against the Sioux and bringing them westward. The Blackfoot and Cree are both Algonkian speakers although have often been enemies to each other. The Blackfoot and Sioux pushed us, the Kootenay, into these mountains. The Stony are also Sioux. North of us, the Cree are Algonkian speakers and they are our allies. I think our language too has Algonkian roots. The Kootenay used to live much of the time on the plains. We only go there now to hunt buffalo. The great herds of buffalo presently live more in our memory than on the prairie. At one time there were buffalo in these mountains providing us with food during the winter."

The words stopped and again Raven was more aware of shadows dancing across rock walls and flickering over the pond's surface. "What's it all about anyway?" asked the raspy voice when starting again. "Like you I've been learning all my life and that's why we come to this earth—to discover through adversity what we can't find and develop from in the spirit side where there are no hard knocks—or arrow shafts below the shoulder. Complain not. Your life is hard because that's why you came here."

"I was foolish to pick such a course," stated Raven.

"I wouldn't walk again along the path I chose," agreed Gray Hawk.

"Who's in charge of it all?" asked Raven.

"The Great Spirit, the Creator," answered Gray Hawk. His and Her presence continues in all creations including wildlife and people. There can be communication between all parts of life because of the common link. Seek this light and that's all we have to do."

"Your words have formed who I am and I will always be grateful," stated Raven.

"You are a healer and a far-seeing person," continued her grandfather.

"I'm going to get some branches to make a bed for sleeping," noted Raven.

"Thank you for your company," said Gray Hawk. She left the cave, returning in a short time to prepare comfortable mats of boughs. Before sleep came, Raven explained, "In the morning I'm going to gather plants and catch fish for our first meal."

The next day when Gray Hawk awoke, light was brightening the cave's entrance along with outlining interior features of walls and telling him trouble was lurking. Knowing the situation involved more than his injury, he was relieved to feel energy surging to meet this challenge as he had met each one in his life. Moving quickly, he gathered his weapons then left the cave, stepping into sunlight that brought no warmth.

He followed Raven's tracks to a place where she had caught fish before shod ponies had arrived bringing boot prints and signs of a struggle. When the horses left, one of them carried an extra rider.

The tracks followed an old trail winding down the mountainside before entering a grove of aspens bordering a stream. Next to the water, the horses were tethered. Smoke from a campfire scented a breeze rustling aspen leaves.

Peering from the surface of water splashing across stones in the stream, Gray Hawk watched the camp. He had placed his bow and arrows on the bank and held his knife while he moved from the water to a tree where Raven was tied.

He had almost finished cutting the bindings when one of the men reached for a rifle and fired, knocking Gray Hawk back into the water. Blood spurted from another wound in his side. The shooter ran forward for a second shot as Raven, broke away from remaining ties, grabbed the knife Gray Hawk had dropped and sank the blade into the attacker's chest.

She picked up his fallen rifle then jumped for the river while shots followed her. From behind the bank, she returned fire, dropping the two shooters. A fourth man fell backwards with an arrow in his forehead.

Raven hugged her grandfather. Following a long interval, she said, "I knew you would come but your arrival even caught me by surprise."

"Surprise wins a battle—usually," he replied.

"Blood," she exclaimed, noticing his reddened chest. "A new wound?"

She applied a band of leather to stop the bleeding before saying, "I have more healing to do."

"Yes," he said. "And I have one more request."

After gathering the prospectors' horses and equipment, Raven and Gray Hawk rode out of the camp.

"Grandfather," said Raven, "will we go home now?"

"Yes," he replied. "You will return first to our village. I will go more directly home. I have seen many winters—you just a few. After more years, you also, like all of us, will go home."

"Can we stop for the night at the old place beside the stream?" she asked again.

"Yes," said Gray Hawk.

"I will check your wounds," added Raven.

Gray Hawk was bent over and not looking well when they reached the old camping location. Raven removed the bullet before adding ointments from herbs to the wounds. Gray Hawk rested while she spitted trout and buffalo meat over a fire.

Following a fine meal, she prepared tea and served it before they both rested while enjoying the drink. Shadows gathered bringing night to their part of the stream beside towering cliffs.

"I have never stopped striving," said Gray Hawk. "As my body grew older, I traveled more in my spirit. I can go back and see the time when we were buffalo hunters and were as free as those we hunted for food. I have always kept the records—the legends—of the Kootenay. These lands are endlessly beautiful. I have seen old people holler with the joy of seeing such places. I can continue to travel among this grandeur in my spirit. I can walk beside the great bear, my totem, whose mark of the paw is on the back of both of my hands. You have the same totem. We are much alike. My journey on this earth stops while your time continues."

The man paused to sip the drink Raven had made. Both man and granddaughter watched the fire brighten before a darkening background. Splashing sounds of the stream were constant while occasionally an owl hooted. Sometimes the fire snapped, sending a trail of sparks to travel upward toward cliffs etched darkly against the night sky where stars sparkled and a red moon shone. A flock of geese, flying lower than adjacent peaks, called to the mountains.

"We are never alone," continued the man. "All of these spirits talk to us and carry a spark of the Great Spirit, the Creator. Soon I will be only in spirit but I, like the others, will not leave you."

"I feel lonely when you talk of keeping me company in spirit because I want you to stay with me physically in addition to the spirit," replied Raven, almost whispering as words traveled clearly in night's calm.

"I've always done the best I could and you can say the same," he explained. "You will carry on my work. Nothing is haphazard. The more I look back at my life the more I am aware of a grand and perfect plan. I struggled with decisions all through the years and, by seeking the Great Spirit, all things work out although the trail traveled seems impossibly wrought with dangers all around and obstacles that seem as tall as our surrounding peaks."

After a short time of rest, listening to the owl again, Gray Hawk said, "Thank you for coming to help me. I always appreciate your work. I notice you have prepared two places with boughs. We can sleep with the companion sound of splashing water. Sleep approaches me. Thank you for helping. I will always be a companion for you."

He walked to the matt of branches and soon gave in to sleep. After checking the camp and looking after the horses, Raven also slept.

The next morning, when first light gave shape to the landscape, Raven stirred from the boughs, stepping into the first flash of sunlight. It brought no brightness or warmth to this morning that for her remained gray when she turned to speak to Gray Hawk and he had gone.

She searched for him, hoping he was in the area but his tracks led toward the adjacent mountainside with its ledges. "You are a very kind man, grandfather," she whispered, looking up at the ledges. "You are like an eagle. You were often on the high places. This time, however, you will only return in spirit. You say we are never alone but I feel lonely. I miss your person-companionship."

In sunlight, Raven started traveling, leading the horses with the supplies back to the village. She stopped once to look back at the ledges among the peaks, knowing her grandfather was there, greeting his spiritual family who had come for him.

Chapter 2

The Drifter

1890

When the Canadian Pacific Railway arrived and established Siding 29 in a place that would be called Banff, the train brought an assortment of passengers and one of them was a drifter. Unlike the railway crews and business people or loggers, miners, prospectors and tourists, one did not fit any of the usual types but had the appearance of a person who would become part of the surrounding mountains, forests, valley and Bow River.

His packs were huge, filled with an assortment of equipment. Noticeable tools were saws, axes, snowshoes and fishing pole. His boots, trousers and shirt were similar to those worn by other workers although the jacket was of fringed leather and the hat appeared to be made of muskrat fur.

The man's brown hair and beard were both long and graying. Facial features were well shaped, showing strength. His black eyes looked out at the world calmly as if, regardless of any raging storm, he, akin to the mountains, would see a better day.

Having left the train, he moved through a flow of people before walking along a dirt street past log buildings. Intrigued by this fellow who did not look similar to the others, a woman, sitting in front of a cabin, asked, "You're not a miner like my father are you?"

"No," he said.

"A logger?" she asked.

"No," he replied again.

"Just traveling through?" came another inquiry.

"Not really through," the stranger said. "I came to live with these mountains."

"Well you've got quite a living partner there," exclaimed the woman. "I hope you're up to it."

"I hope I'm up to it too," said the stranger, "but I think I'm home."

"Mister, you have a beautiful home," stated the woman. "I don't want to be a bother but, right now, you're my only target. What's your name?"

"Charlie James," came the answer. After turning long enough to state his name, he for the first time glanced at the young woman sitting on the step of a log cabin. Her clothes were plain yet well-scrubbed and this was the first really clean clothing other than his own he had seen for a long time. Shortly cropped blonde hair bordered the woman's beautiful face. Her sparkling eyes were blue.

"I have to ask," he explained, "why would a flower like you grow in this place?"

"I rent rooms," she answered. "My father builds the cabins when he's not in the mine. Much of my work is cooking along with sewing people back together when they get injured."

"This place needs you," exclaimed Charlie.

"I'm Barb Sims," she said. "Good to meet you."

"Good to know you," countered Charlie.

He kept walking while Barb reached for a cup on the roughly hewn steps. After finishing the remnant of cold tea she whispered, "Something tells me I just met a man I'm going to be hearing from often. The railway is bringing new times to this river valley."

Charlie stopped. The image of the beautiful woman in scrubbed clothes was in his thoughts when he looked ahead and got another glimpse of the panorama before him. Sunlight emblazoned snow-capped peaks above verdant slopes touched by a blue tinge that deepened with distance. Equal in vastness, the sky was also predominantly blue although laced with clouds painted golden by sunlight. There was stillness to the scene making it seem unreal like a mirage he had dreamed about so often he could at any time conjure up a picture. Now the scene before him was real just as its call to him—a message from a place where he could rest.

"I'm here now," he confirmed. *I have much to see—much to learn and if I've learned one thing about myself I know all knowledge will be acquired the hard way. I have much to do before I rest tonight. I've traveled further today because I've started and that's always the longest stretch of the trail.*

Hours later, he halted his journey, looked around at the surrounding landscape and thought, *I've walked from sunrise toward sunset and the view does not seem to have changed as if the scenery moves ahead the same distance as each step I take. I'm in a land of giants where mountains tower above clouds and river valleys are vast while the sky provides an endless, encircling panorama.*

I have come to a stream providing fresh water and a good place to camp for the night, he decided before removing his packs. He placed them inside a quickly assembled lean-to topped by a tarpaulin.

Time to wash away some weariness, he declared before removing most of his clothes then wading into the stream. At first the water felt chilling and hostile. Gradually he adjusted after he stretched out in the stream with just his face above the surface.

Banff

Flowing water massaged tired muscles, reviving them while he watched the sky. Like clouds drifting in darkening hues from the late afternoon sun, his thoughts wandered before coming to rest with the blonde hair, blue eyes and beauty of Barb. *She seemed to be experienced and tough, not at all hesitant about talking to and questioning a stranger*, he recalled. *She must greet new people every day. She was direct, showing strength she would need to possess in this land where power prevails along with adaptability. Delicate features have to adapt to survive, as do flowers or chickadees.*

Suddenly, the sky darkened, sending Charlie's muscles into a knot of alarm. A light-blocking form towering overhead took the shape of a moose. The closest parts were whiskers where droplets of water hung, remnants of a refreshing drink the giant had just enjoyed from the stream. After both forest residents identified each other, the moose walked away, unblocking the sky. Charlie stood up and watched the cow moose with her calf move out of view beyond foliage.

Heat from a fire was soothing. After drying, he replaced his clothes then walked downstream until he came to a pool.

He dropped in a fishing line and hook, baited with a strip of bacon. Quickly he caught two trout. He spit them over the fire before enjoying a fine meal followed by tea.

It's a privilege to live in such a majestic place, he thought while the campfire's flames brightened in contrast to deepening shadows of night. *Moose live here and leave no damage behind along their back trails. Humans are the only residents who bring wreckage. Some change is needed for inclusions such as a railway and settlement at Banff. However, we can live together without destroying our surroundings, bringing harm to everything including ourselves. We have a habit of promoting our own achievements while overlooking the gifts of others. Large animals live here without leaving behind marks of their presence except trails that often establish routes followed by Indigenous people then much later by Europeans. European explorers have recently arrived in this country and while they are discovering a new place they overlook the fact they had an Indigenous guide to show them where everything is located and has been enjoyed for thousands of years yet kept in such pristine condition the Europeans* thought *they were in a new land—and discovered it. There has been an appalling disregard for the traditions of the Indigenous people.*

Charlie welcomed the new day by making coffee and having a first meal of dried meat and bannock. When he was ready to leave camp he looked at the surrounding vistas and said to himself, *this land is going to be my new home. Therefore I want to understand it, check its trails and visit the mountains along with streams. I'll get to know every aspect of this landscape's beauty while at the same time find my place to build a cabin.*

With a plan prepared, he started to walk. Each trail followed, every creek crossed or valley entered became part of a map he stored in his memory until the region, with its towering majesty of mountains and wide sweep of valleys, formed in his recollection a storehouse of unlimited grandeur.

At one of his camps, he declared to himself, *all of the grandeur I have seen must be shared with others. After I build my cabin, I'll become a guide to show other people some of the magnificence I have seen. I'll share the beauty but only with those who do it no harm. The Bow River Valley is a center in this landscape as are the mountains. Additionally, though there are unlimited numbers of smaller vistas with streams and lakes—those original or pristine features that can bring any visitor to a glimpse beyond the physical realm to the spiritual side, providing an opportunity to climb and transcend to a higher view of life. After such a journey, the problems of life fade away. My new purpose will be to take tourists on excursions to what can only be the Creator's garden and here there continues real life from the presence of the Creator.*

Charlie had just determined his new role when he walked into what seemed to be a natural clearing. He stood on an elevated section of smooth rock. The site overlooked a gently sloping path to a river. Beyond it, in a sweeping panorama, there were mountains.

I feel like I've been here before, he thought, after he sat down and leaned his back against a pine trunk. *I could sit here forever, without moving like the rocks, trees or mountains. When I'm in the right place—this perfect location—there is no need, and I have no desire, to move away. I'm home.*

Having watched the scene before him until evening shadows reminded him of approaching night, Charlie resolved, *obviously this is home and here I'll build my cabin. With the money I've saved, I'll go to Banff and have supplies brought here by packhorses. After I get someone to bring in equipment, I'll get started assembling logs. I'll select them from places where removal does no harm.*

He walked to Siding 29, now called Banff. Businesses were getting started in log and sometimes board structures and he purchased items for the construction of a cabin. He also arranged to have everything delivered by an outfitter.

With the work completed, he had sufficient funds to celebrate with a meal at the saloon. The interior of the building was as rough, yet sturdy, as the logs used for construction. He sat beside a table providing a view of a shadowy room where three men were drinking at another table and kept the proprietor busy.

Every aspect of the saloon owner revealed strength. His torso was as thick and straight as a tree trunk and arms were akin to matching branches. The available meal was stew so Charlie, after pretending to weigh the choice carefully, informed the man who, during the introduction, said his name was Syd Cleever, "I think I'll have the stew."

"Good choice," confirmed Syd, cracking a smile that apparently did not appear often on his whiskered face where a tangle of graying hair was just controlled sufficiently to reveal gray eyes that looked out at the world with confidence.

"I'm a miner," offered Syd. "Coal miner. Saved enough money to start this saloon. Trains need coal for steam but miners need food too. After workin' in a mine, I enjoy a good meal and seldom got one so I learned how to cook—nothin' fancy. And bread goes with the stew."

"Good," declared Charlie. "Bread and stew are the best foods a person could get—along with beans and coffee."

"You can have beans and coffee too," offered Syd. "I didn't mention beans because that's a standard—so is the coffee."

"I like this place already," declared Charlie. "I used my cash for supplies. Do you accept gold for payment?"

"I hope you become a regular customer," answered Syd. "Are you a prospector?"

"You were a miner before getting established with a saloon and I did some prospecting. I panned enough to begin life in these mountains."

"What work are you goin' to do now," asked Syd.

"Build a cabin then start guiding," he answered.

"Good choices," confirmed Syd. "I'll get your food."

When the stew, bread, beans and coffee arrived, Charlie savored the most delicious meal he had enjoyed since the earlier days at the farm before his parents were taken by cholera. To Syd who appeared occasionally from the kitchen Charlie said, "I'm pleased you left the mines to become a cook because that's the finest meal I've enjoyed since I was back at the family farm."

"Thank you," he replied. "I make what I like. As I said, after a day's work, I wanted good food so had to start makin' it myself. Nothin' fancy, though."

"Cooking like that is as hard to come by as a nugget in a pan," added Charlie.

"We're prospectors too," said one of the three men who had finished their drinks at the other table.

"I'm Reg," continued the same man as the three approached. Charlie could smell them as they sat around his table after dragging over chairs. "This is Len," Reg added, indicating another guy then pointing to the third, "and Case." The men wore soiled clothes, were unshaven—similarly scruffy.

Alike too was their way of smirking and glancing at each other appearing to share information only they knew. This aspect bonded them together providing courage they would lack separately.

"We haven't struck any new finds lately but we're always lookin'," explained Reg.

And you're looking now thought Charlie, who was repulsed by their stink and jeering presence.

Approaching from the kitchen, Syd loomed over the table and with mock politeness said, "Forgive me if I offend. But you three gentlemen have drinks to pay for."

Len and Case glanced at Reg—who put money on the table. Syd removed the cash then returned to the kitchen.

"We have a new stream we're panning now," offered Reg. "Are you working around here?"

"No," said Charlie. "I just arrived from back east."

"You looked like a tenderfoot," said Reg, continuing to exchange glances and smirks with the other two.

"I don't need company," stated Charlie, no longer able to tolerate the stink or the hostility.

"You don't like our company?" asked Reg.

"I didn't ask for it," countered Charlie.

"You're just plain lucky," continued Reg. "You got our company and you found some nuggets."

"I'm about to use the nugget," explained Charlie. He stood up and walked to the bar as the three men left the building.

Approaching, Syd said, "Sorry about the riffraff." Receiving the nugget, he continued, "That will keep you in food here for a long time. I'll let you know if it runs out."

"You and your food make up for the riffraff," confirmed Charlie. "Such good food is hard to find. The riffraff are more common."

"Thanks," replied Syd. "See you soon."

"Been a pleasure," added Charlie before he left the building.

When he stepped outside, he was hit on the head. A light flashed in his mind and he struggled to stay conscious, knowing he was in trouble. Something slammed into the side of his face. He just realized the object was a knife when Syd appeared. He picked up one attacker in each hand, dragged them to a trough and threw them in. Charlie added the third.

"They needed some cleaning," stated Syd.

"By the smell o' 'em, that's their first one," said Charlie. "Thanks for your help. They almost turned out my lights."

"I was on the lookout for trouble," stated Syd. "Aside from the stink o' 'em, they also smelled of trouble. They're the types that don't attack head on. I have to bat around customers all the time."

"Appreciate your help," affirmed Charlie.

"See Barb up the street," continued Syd. "She patches up my customers and you have a bad knife wound."

"Good advice," replied Charlie. "I'll go there now."

Walking toward the place where he had talked to the woman, Charlie was suddenly aware of a throbbing headache. Feeling the back of his head, his hand came away without blood yet there was quite a lump where he had been hit. His face bled more slowly and for the first time he noticed the blood on his coat.

At the log building, there was no one present. He walked to the side then followed a path leading toward cabins. Hearing sounds coming from the first structure, he looked through an open doorway and saw the woman washing something on a scrub board.

Turning, she recognized him and said, "Been getting acquainted have you?"

"Yes," he answered. "I've been out making new friends in the community."

"There are good people here," she replied. "Did you meet any of them?"

"Yes," he said. "Syd Cleever."

"He's a good one," she confirmed. "They don't come any stronger."

"I noticed," said Charlie. "He threw two men into a horse trough. I just tossed in one—Reg, Len and Case."

"Washing them was a good idea," she added as her face brightened with a smile. "They attacked you?"

"Yes," he answered.

"Watch them," she warned. "They're rats you won't know are around until they strike. I've patched up some of those they've robbed."

"They've sent you another customer," he added, turning his face to show her the wound.

"A knife?" she asked.

"Yes," he said.

After preparing a cloth in the tub, she placed this warm, soapy material over the cut before saying, "Hold that in place."

Using a second, cleaning cloth, she scrubbed blood from his coat. "We'll go up to the other cabin," she directed.

She led the way to the front building, opened its door and both went inside. With Charlie sitting on a chair beside a table, Barb walked to a cupboard then withdrew one of a line of bottles. "My father makes home brew and I often get paid with the stuff although I rarely drink it," she explained. "I use it to clean injuries and to help with pain."

Pouring some of this liquid over the cut, she caught extra drops with a cloth before she filled a small glass and gave it to Charlie, saying, "This will help with what I'm about to do."

After pouring extra brew into a dish, she soaked a needle and thread. Displaying experience, her hands moved quickly and brought the needle toward Charlie's face.

He drank the brew, feeling the flame enter his body and numbing him. Barb pierced his skin with the needle. Next an extended, searing torment followed the course of the first closure on the cut.

"You're tough," exclaimed Barb. "So is your hide," she added, starting another join.

"Will I be pretty when you're finished?" he asked.

"Just gorgeous," she exclaimed, laughing. "Around here beauty is in the mountains, valleys, rivers and even inside some of the people. You have your share."

"You have it inside and outside," he observed.

"I'm surprised you can say that with the pain I'm giving you," she noted.

"You're patching me," he countered. "I appreciate your work. It's painful but that's the way I do all things—the hard way."

"Life is hard—for most people," she stated after she cut off the thread. "The faster we learn that the more successful we'll be. Your cut has been closed." Having applied a finishing coating of home brew to the wound, she asked, "Want more to drink?"

"The first drink was enough," he answered as he withdrew a knife from the table and started to cut thread closing a layer of material on his coat. He removed a gold nugget and gave it to her. "Thank you for your help. This is some coming back to you from all you send out."

"Such help is more than you received," she declared, holding the heavy item.

"I appreciate your work," he explained. "I struggled for years in preparation to come here. I knew I would need cash to get started. Now new projects will begin."

"Excitement comes with starting," offered Barb, as she looked through the adjacent window providing a view of mountains. "People find this to be a harsh place—a land of cold water and rock. Seekers often see what's inside them—and not what's outside. This landscape has beauty, not just in one part, but also in aspects that are intricately woven together in a tapestry—a pageantry of life that has majesty and grandeur beyond our most wondrous dreams. Only a pristine wilderness is truly wild—the purest expression of the Creator's handiwork. To the extent we can see the wild is our progress in our struggle to develop. Some people, like Reg, Len and Case see only cold water and rock because that's in themselves and they have deliberately turned away."

"Wow," exclaimed Charlie, "you can see a long way."

"There's a lot to admire in this landscape," continued Barb. "Banff is small now; however, people are attracted to this place. They come for the tonic of such magnificent scenery and for the medicine of the hot springs. Visitors—tourists—will arrive just to see beauty yet the best part is the opportunity to compare their inside advancement to the measuring gage of wild—and wild is here. Banff is starting to be protected so that people will always be able to come here for this highest experience. In a city, there is beauty in people. We have that in Banff too plus much more—the pristine wilderness."

"You really believe in this place, don't you," he said.

"I can see what's here—beauty—true wilderness," she added before turning away from the window and appreciating the strength she saw in him. "You already know life is hard so that part won't deter you. You'll be remembered."

"Today, I thought I'd just take a short journey into Banff and had no idea I would actually travel so far," he exclaimed.

"And you've just started," she added.

"I have a cabin to build," he noted. "I've arranged for supplies to be delivered."

"You've made a good start by meeting Syd Cleever but watch out for the other three," she said. "They're the most dangerous when you don't see them."

"Good advice," he confirmed, before walking to the doorway. "I look forward to seeing you again."

"Be careful out there," she noted before he left and she returned to her work.

After going back to his building site, Charlie resumed the project of gathering logs. First cutting, trimming and, as much as possible, peeling them, he next used a rope to haul each one to be ready for construction. Pleased with the log preparations, he finished an outhouse then placed the foundation logs.

As with every part of his life he threw himself into each task, letting it envelope him. He stopped for meals only if necessary and did not rest unless exhaustion kept him from proceeding. He was a bit surprised when packhorses arrived led by an outfitter accompanied by Syd Cleever.

"Welcome Syd," exclaimed Charlie, pleased to see this man who had become a friend.

"I help people in the community and I wanted to see your building site," replied Syd. "Your location is beautiful and the log cabin will be too. In this country the scenery makes the home. You're off to a great start. The outfitter here is Isaac Thomas." Isaac was a slim, muscular man with well—tanned face and light brown eyes along with a smile seeming to reflect an optimistic outlook on life.

"Good to meet you," replied Charlie.

"And you too," said Isaac as they shook hands. "Syd speaks well of you and you can't get a better introduction than that."

"He just keeps being a great contributor," noted Charlie. "He helped me wash a few guys."

"A lot o' 'em could use it," observed Isaac, laughing.

"These three guys insisted on getting washed," explained Charlie.

"A lot o' 'em do that too," added Isaac. "I'll get started unpacking and taking care of the horses. There's a lot to do."

Before nightfall, the supplies had been unloaded with items needing protection from the weather stored in a tent. Another tent was established for Charlie's headquarters. Here the three men prepared bough mattresses for sleeping during the night.

Over a fire, Syd roasted steaks on spits. "I prefer to cook steaks without using a pan because it sears and toughens the meat's surface," he explained. "You'll notice the tenderness."

Later, when the three men were enjoying the meal, Charlie said, "This steak is so delicious it reminds me of my home at the farm when I was a kid."

"I knew they'd be the best," agreed Isaac. "I've enjoyed Syd's steaks during other trips. You're the finest cook. Good thing you stopped mining."

"I like preparing food," observed Syd. "I also did not approve of what mining does to the land and water. Trains need coal; so I suppose mining is necessary."

"Along the same course, you also only serve beef in your saloon," noted Isaac.

"Yes," agreed Syd. "Wild game is part of the wilderness. Cattle are raised for food. If people don't have a choice, that's a different situation. I have a choice."

"You choose outstanding food," stated Charlie.

"The best I've ever experienced," added Isaac.

"Time has come for my meal finisher," said Syd, as he opened a bottle. "This is my special home brew—made it myself."

"You're an amazing host," said Charlie. "I'll have to follow some of your methods."

"It's because of you we're here," countered Syd before he poured the drinks. Raising his glass, he proclaimed, "Here's to your new home and life in the Banff wilderness—a place where anyone can measure his or her own spirit compared to the magnificence of a true wilderness. It too has a spirit. A spirit lives in these mountains. Banff is a spiritual place."

Charlie was caught by the spell of the scene with the fire where tall flames danced before a dark background etched against a pale sky brightened by stars and a half moon. Flames jumped light across the forms of new—yet old—friends.

In the morning the fire was rekindled for preparations of flapjacks and coffee. Before departure, Syd said, "I didn't realize how much fun delivering supplies could be."

"I always enjoy being an outfitter," agreed Isaac. "This trip though has been special."

"I'm going to miss you guys," said Charlie. "Strange to think, a short time ago I had not met you or been to this location where I feel so much at home."

"A great start like this foretells you are at the beginning of an outstanding journey—and I'm going to be hearing about your story often," stated Syd.

"We all have lots of work to do," noted Isaac before they started the horses on the return trip.

"Thanks for your help and a wonderful beginning," Charlie called out before his friends moved away.

First he added improvements to his tent camp. He needed them for the snow that whitened the landscape for the next few days. Snow on the ground helped to slide logs into place. He also could stay warm by sawing, chopping and hammering during each day and often at night.

After the first logs were in place, topped by boards brought in by packhorse, the stove was added followed by a fireplace. River stones were used and sealed with mortar until a finished structure was ready for testing. A small flame swarmed along shavings then among split wood before climbing onto logs and gathering into a blaze drawn by a strong draft upward into the chimney.

"The fireplace works," he declared while watching the draft draw the flames. A good source of heat is so important. I think I'll celebrate by going fishing."

Charlie sent his baited line into the stream and, in a short time, caught two trout for an evening meal. While preparing the fish for spitting over a fire he thought, *maybe I should build an elevated cache so I can store fish along with other frozen food.*

During the next few days, a pulley system helped to put into place vertical logs to support the construction of a storage chamber. A ladder was built to establish the flooring topped by support walls and roof. When the really cold weather arrived, food was cached safely along with a good supply of fish.

The firm grip of winter accompanied the raising of the cabin's walls. Raven visitors to the new home enjoyed food put out for them on a raised platform. A pair of coyotes came to another location where food was provided. Elk left tracks, occasionally, in the area, as did mule deer, moose, snowshoe hares, red squirrels, muskrats and beaver. Less frequent visitors were gray wolves and lynx. A mountain lion left a trail of prints once. Bird neighbors were great horned owls, ptarmigan, spruce grouse, ruffed grouse, crows, chickadees and Canada jays. Ducks and geese frequented open water along the river.

Of numerous forest dwellers, those that made the log cabin part of their lives were a pair of coyotes along with foxes and snowshoe hares. They accepted Charlie although used timeless techniques in being wary of other forest inhabitants. Winter birds usually were present every day as were ravens, Canada jays and crows. Calls of owls accompanied the nights.

I enjoy the owl's call thought Charlie, after the wild voice greeted him again. Sleep usually came easily to Charlie's tired muscles.

Mornings seemed to be the coldest part of a day and the chill lasted until the stove brought more heat to the tent. Warmth returned during the preparation of breakfast involving some variation of flapjacks, bannock, fried potatoes or beans.

When the walls were in place along with doors and windows Charlie celebrated by going fishing before breakfast. He returned with a trout and added it to some fried potatoes to accompany the usual coffee.

Time is an elusive thing, he mused while resting beside his fire in front of the building site. *The more I'm in charge of my own time the more I'm short of it and always hurrying. Likely that's why I enjoy these moments of rest required to build up a supply of energy for the next project.*

Hearing resonant calls ringing through frosty stillness, Charlie thought, *I'm pleased ravens have become regular companions. Coyotes also have added this place to their route. They have accepted me as a friendly part of their lives. As I see those more frequently, I notice how they enjoy each other's company. These coyotes are almost always together and like to chase each other. The male is larger and taller than the female. They like the food I leave for them, as do the ravens. Now that the coyotes are here more often, I don't see the foxes as often.*

After refilling his coffee cup, he observed, *the snow helps to slide logs. I'm now working on the upper part of the structure above any accumulation of snow. By spring I should have this cabin completed. Isaac and Syd brought in all needed supplies. With the arrival of spring, more tourists will be returning and I'll be ready to start guiding. I now know the region and can set up a comfortable camp. I wouldn't guide loggers but they don't use help anyway. The clear-cutting that has been done leaves an ugly scar on the land. Erosion has been ruining streams. We should enjoy what is here rather than cut or shoot it then remove part of the wilderness. Hunting is a traditional method of getting food if such food is required. Killing for sport, unneeded food or trophies is a crime. I'd better get back to work.*

Charlie notched the next log or trimmed a board and put them in place as the structure grew to a log shell. With the fireplace providing warmth, the interior became an easier work area. Tables were formed in addition to chairs before beds were completed for a room in the loft and two on the main floor.

The cabin was almost finished by the arrival of spring and the next person to arrive. Charlie had started breakfast when a rider slid from the back of her horse and waved before leading the pinto to water for a drink. After tying her horse in an area of new grass, she removed packs and saddle. "She's not just my horse," she said to Charlie, "she is my friend."

"This is a land of surprises," replied Charlie, almost whispering, "but none of them match the incredible sight and happiness of seeing you here."

"That's better than hearing you're too busy for visitors," she said.

"Well now that you mention it, I am sort of—" he replied. "You're always welcome. Timing is right too. Come and have breakfast."

Bringing Barb a chair, he said, "Maybe you could place that where you can get the best view."

She sat down and sipped coffee before saying, "No one had heard from you all winter. I had to know if you were well or needed help. I brought supplies I thought you could use—such as coffee."

"The best you can bring is your company," he exclaimed. "I still can't believe such a wonderful occurrence as having you here."

"Good to see you too," she countered, "and you seem well."

"Have worked all winter on the cabin," he explained.

"You have not marred this magnificent region," she observed while glancing at the structure. "Your home fits—blends in."

"Are you still renting cabins?" he asked.

"Yes," she answered. "Before the season got busier, I thought I would drop by for a visit with you. I'm going to do some work with the outfitter, Isaac Thomas. He said when he's guiding tourists he could use help with any medical situations that arise along with cooking, setting up camp and packing. I rent cabins so this fits with outfitting. I'll send you tourists for guiding."

"Thank you," he replied. "I'm going to be a guide—but not for hunters."

"I'm not in charge of Isaac's trips but if I were, I wouldn't take tourists hunting either."

"Seeing you sitting beside the fire seems as natural as the surrounding landscape," he observed.

"Feels natural to be here," she added.

"I'll serve you breakfast," he said before getting up and resuming his work around the fire.

Barb sipped the warm drink while Charlie finished preparations. A flock of geese flew past. They were high in the sky yet their calls carried to the land and rang with apparent excitement which they likely felt while returning to their spring, summer and fall homes.

"As I mentioned before," said Barb after Charlie served flapjacks accompanied by fried potatoes and bannock, "my horse, Scout, is not just transportation. She is my friend. Too many people treat horses and other animals as things instead of living creatures. More people see dogs as friends—and the bond is as strong as or stronger than between people. The Indian beliefs say all things have a spirit. Who could tell us that the geese honking during their passage northward are not enjoying life? All this is why, like you, I'm against hunting unless food is not just used but needed. This meal by the way is delicious."

"Kind of you to say so," countered Charlie. "Syd is a great cook and he said you are too. Isaac knows of your cooking skills and is lucky to have your help. There's so much to do, people like us are always busy. Did you have any trouble finding this place?"

"Could not have been easier," she exclaimed. "I'm not visiting you in your home. You are visiting me in my home. When Syd told me where you were located, I couldn't believe it. I come to this location all the time. You notice there was a fire pit where your fire now burns. I come here, build a fire and rest before returning to work. I have always considered this place to be home."

"Wow," he whispered. "I had the same feeling when I first arrived and knew the cabin would be at this location. Great to have you present. Hopefully you will return often."

"I always have," she answered. "As I mentioned, I brought you fresh provisions. After this meal, I'll unpack them."

"Your company is all you have to bring," he said. "Amazing to hear this is your favorite place too. The people of Banff live apart in land distance but close personally. In a large town or city people live closer territorially yet further apart personally. When I'm working, I enjoy the company of friends in Banff although they are a long walk or ride away."

"I like your cabin," noted Barb. "You've been busy."

"I always seem to be in a hurry and only rest when I'm too tired to continue," he reflected.

"Welcome to the new community of Banff," she proclaimed. "At least that's the case for those who work honestly. Some seek a life without work—such as many wealthy tourists or guys such as those who cut your face. They are only a threat to you when you don't see them."

"Your stitches fixed my face," he noted.

"They should have been removed long ago," she explained. "I'll take them out after unpacking. Fried potatoes are always good. You make superb bannock. I like having someone else do the cooking."

"That does make the food taste better," he added before following her to the supplies. They were stored in the cabin while Barb observed the new structure.

"Your building is a natural part of these mountains," she exclaimed after all items had been neatly stored. She sat down while Charlie kindled a fire in the new river stone fireplace. Looking around, she said, "A place that rings with life like the bugle of an elk—a celebration."

"You have a special way of seeing things," he noted.

"You supply such a tonic—you and your cabin," she said. "Both seem natural as if you've always been here."

"I seemed to recognize this site when I arrived," he observed.

"I had the same impression. Maybe this is a good time to remove those stitches. As I mentioned, they should've been taken out earlier. That was a deep gash and had to be closed. I'll leave the bottle of brew I'll use in case you require patching again or get thirsty."

After fist soaking the wound along with a small knife, Barb was removing the stitching when Charlie was struck by her beauty. She finished, put away her equipment and left the building.

She was leading her horse but stopped to enjoy the sweeping grandeur of river, forest, mountains and cabin. Charlie stepped in front of this background. He put one arm on her shoulder then his other arm on her opposite side before slowly moving forward to a lengthy embrace. He had time to open his eyes, see her eyes—lashes and face surrounded by blonde hair with a backdrop of pine branches.

Before she rode away, she turned toward him and said, "Isaac and Syd didn't warn me about that part of the visit."

"Hopefully you will return," he replied.

"I seem to have never left," she added.

She rode away but the memory of her presence fueled Charley for the work of finishing the building then preparing to be a guide.

Chapter 3

The Guide

Barb returned to Charlie's cabin with news she had tourists waiting to be guided. She led a second horse for Charlie to ride back with her.

In Banff, she introduced him to Ben and Alice Rollins. They wore clothing of the latest style from boots to hats, looking as two people modeling equipment rather than actual travelers wanting to hike in the wilderness without its risks. Ben was well shaved with the rest of his face without apparent blemish. Alice mirrored his good looks with added fragility. Ben's closely cropped hair was brown and his wife was blonde.

"We're ready to be off," Ben said to Charlie after introductions had been made and Barb had left the three travelers to begin their journey.

"We're leaving right away," replied Charlie before he turned northward and started walking toward the Bow River.

"Our information says Lake Louise was first called by the Indians, Lake of Little Fishes," noted Alice.

"Yes," confirmed Charlie.

"And it was discovered by Thomas Wilson who was part of the Canadian Pacific Railway crew at Kicking Horse Pass," continued Alice. "He found the lake in 1882."

"He discovered it," said Charlie, "and the Stonys, particularly one man called Edwin Hunter showed him where it was."

"The name, Louise," noted Alice, "comes from Queen Victoria's daughter, Princess Louise Caroline Alberta."

"Past information helps us know the present," added Charlie.

"Banff gets its name from Banffshire, the Scottish birthplace of Canadian Pacific Railway president, George Stephen," stated Alice.

"You're actually the guide here," exclaimed Charlie. "Thanks for the tour."

Banff

"The tour continues," declared Alice. "Banff Park started in 1885 by the Federal Government as a twenty six square kilometer reserve to protect Cave, Basin and Upper Hot Springs. In 1887 the area expanded to six hundred and seventy three kilometers in the formation of the Rocky Mountains Park Reserve, a joint Venture of the Canadian Pacific Railway and Federal Government, all confirmed by the Rocky Mountains Park Act. In 1886 construction started for the Banff Springs Hotel where we are staying. It was just completed."

"Have enjoyed your tour," said Charlie. "The past explains today."

"I'm here to see a grizzly," announced Ben. To Charlie, he added, "You're here to give me confidence that I'm the tourist looking for the bear and the bear isn't the tourist looking for me."

"Bears along with all wildlife usually respond to you as you treat them," confirmed Charlie. "Alice has been guiding us through what has been established recently. People have been coming to this Bow River Valley for thousands of years and surrounding nations include this land in traditional stories. People came to meet, trade and get food. The hot springs were considered medicinal and used for healing."

Stopping at a clearing on a point overlooking the river valley, Charlie said, "You should look at this scene with the wide, peaceful river flowing through a vista of grandeur where forested slopes rise beyond the clouds to peaks topped in ice and snow, shining in sunlight through all the seasons of the year. Such a scene you can hold in your memory then revisit this place in times of stress to remind yourself goodness of life is greater than hard times you are experiencing. The spirit that's more visible here also helps, supports and walks with you."

"Let's stay a long time," whispered Ben before he and Alice sat down. "I don't want to miss what's here."

"I guided us with facts and information," observed Alice, "but Charlie guides us to why we came here before we even knew ourselves. Now I know why I wanted to see Banff. It's more than hot springs and a place for wealthy tourists to visit. This location starts with the healing powers of the hot springs the Indian nations first visited but greater healing comes from the unusual magnificence of the region. In such beauty, we more easily not only see but also feel a spiritual presence of the Creator. This place is not a park. It's a spirit. It's uplifting. At first I found joy in our new clothes and luxurious hotel with its delicious food. Those pleasures are diminished though by the magnificence Charlie has guided us to behold. I see it, feel it. It fills me. The memory of such a place I'll always cherish, particularly in those times when I feel down. I guided us with facts while Charlie has shown us why everyone should come here."

"Up ahead, a cold mountain stream provides excellent water for our camp," suggested Charlie before he led the way along a trail used for thousands of years by both people and wildlife.

Charlie stopped, as did Ben and Alice. Ahead, at the top of a hill, there stood a grizzly. The sentinel clawed the air as if checking for a sign. As was everything else in the region, the bear was massive with an immense head, wide shoulders and deeply furred hide covering powerful muscles.

With surprising agility for its size, the bear started walking forward. Furred sides glistened as muscles bunched and flowed, bringing danger closer to the three people.

"That's why we wanted a guide," whispered Ben to Charlie. "We wanted to see this land yet such beauty must be explored respectfully. Mistakes in a great land can also be large. Here we don't want to make a mistake."

Increasing speed to a slow lope, the form advanced, narrowing the distance to the people. The closer the grizzly came, the faster it moved. In front of Charlie, the bear stopped then stood, appearing to be even more massive at close range.

Charlie raised his arm and looked directly at the standing form. The eyes were brown.

"Follow me as we move off the trail," whispered Charlie before all three people stepped out of the way of the grizzly.

The great bear resumed walking along the path and soon moved out of view. "That was like a large chunk of mountain," said Ben.

"We'll never forget this trip," exclaimed Alice.

"Thanks for not running," said Charlie.

"I thought of it," admitted Alice. "But where would we go? We could never run fast enough. You didn't run and you're our guide."

"Smartest thing we ever did was get Charlie James for our guide," added Ben. "He has shown us Banff and we'll never forget such a story."

"Ahead we can camp," noted Charlie as he resumed traveling.

At a site sheltered by rocks and pines yet providing a panoramic view of the area, Charlie set up a lean-to. To its top, he added a tarp. In front of this structure he kindled a fire. When he returned from fishing in a pool downstream, he spitted trout over the fire. He served this delicacy along with fried potatoes and beans followed by tea.

Sitting beside the fire while evening shadows deepened as night arrived, Alice said, "In the shortest time we've had the grandest experience."

"Outfitters with horses provide longer excursions," observed Charlie. "Short experiences can be long in enjoyment."

"And always remembered," exclaimed Alice.

The next people Charlie was called upon to guide were Ed and Sonya Conley. In appearance, they were opposites. He was short, wiry and seemed to be always moving. His eyes were brown as was his hair although it was also quite gray. His wife, Sonya was comparatively tall and seemed to be almost as wide. Width, however, came with strength. Her eyes were black and hair, shortly cropped, was the same color with added brown blends.

"We're here to go fishing," stated Ed by way of introduction. "I needed some luxury for Sonya so we're staying at the Banff Springs Hotel. I aim to go fishing."

"That's our plan," replied Charlie as he started walking toward the Bow River. "I'm going to take you to the one place where you have the greatest chance of catching the best fish in the shortest time."

"That's exactly what we want and everyone we talked to recommended you," replied Ed.

"Right at the start," said Sonya, "I'd like to alert you, Charlie, to Ed's tendency to get injured so today we can have fun without him losing any more of his parts. One time we were trawling for bass and the motor got sluggish. Ed's a maintenance mechanic. He's best at what he does. He can listen to a motor and determine how its functioning can be improved. This ability to trouble shoot saves companies much money. When we were bass fishing, he realized what was wrong with the motor and started removing weeds from the prop. Blades from the propeller cut off two of his fingers. He has been around motors so much he sometimes forgets they are not his friends like animals or birds would be if you knew and cared so much about them."

The travelers walked in silence the rest of the way to a bend in the Bow River where the current rippled the surface and Charlie knew this was the best place to catch a large fish in a short time. Sonya sat down to relax while enjoying surrounding grandeur while Charlie started a fire and prepared to make coffee.

"He has just learned to fly fish," Sonya informed Charlie; before Ed initiated his technique for sending an artificial fly he had tied himself out to attract the first fish. The pole, like something alive, whipped the fly back and forth. When it was behind Ed, it was turned then sent forward smacking him in the back of his head.

"Nice work Ed," screamed Sonya, laughing. "You caught something big on your first cast."

Subdued, Ed stepped ashore and held the line while Charlie cut it, leaving a small piece dangling from the fly in his skin.

"I can pull the hook forward, bring it through the rest of the way," explained Charlie. "After I cut off the barb, I'll pull the metal back out the way it went in. I prepare for injuries by bringing a bottle of home brew. I'll pour some on the cut and your wound should heal quickly. Maybe you should wear a hat when you're fly fishing."

"He needs more than a hat to keep him from getting injured," jabbed Sonya.

Charlie quickly tended to the injury. In a short time, Ed tied on another fly then waded out again into the stream. He brought the pole back to life and this time successfully sent a fly out onto the river's surface. After letting the decoy move downstream, the pole again brought the bait back. It was on the way out again across the water when Ed stepped into a deep area and went under. He thrashed wildly while Charlie helped him to secure footing.

"The score is two nothing for the fish," shouted Sonya, as Charlie returned to the bank.

"Water's cold," declared Charlie. "Takes a dedicated fisherman to swim in there."

"Hope he doesn't lose any more of his parts," she replied.

"Coffee will soon be ready," observed Charlie when he sat down beside her to watch what had become a tranquil scene with the river swirling smoothly past, topped occasionally by a colorful bit of feather and fur Ed had tied around a hook to attract a fish.

Spray shot from the surface in a crest of silver emblazoned in sunlight, above the leaping form of the largest rainbow trout any of them had previously seen. Ed hollered with excitement as he pulled back on the pole to set the hook and a battle started. He was backing up when he went under the surface. Thrashing with one arm while the other held the pole, the wildly excited man received support from Charlie. Struggling to stay above the surface did not distract Ed's focus on catching this fish. Again it shot from the river, sending another crest of droplets into sunlight, before returning to murky depths.

Ed hollered with pure joy while the fish fought. Gradually it came to the river's bank where Ed held up his catch so Sonya could take pictures.

"Great work Ed," shouted Sonya. "You achieved your dream."

"A wonderful dream has come true here in this magnificent country," he declared. "I've caught a fish equal to all of it. This trout is too great for fillets. We have pictures and I've had some of the most fun I've ever had. The fish that has given me so much is too important for fillets. He placed the rainbow trout in the water and watched happily as the dark form became again part of the river.

"You should get warm and dry beside this fire," suggested Charlie. "I've braced your coffee with some home brew."

Receiving a cup from Charlie, Ed sipped some of the dark liquid and declared, "This is one of the best days of my life and, as they said at the hotel, 'Charlie James is the guide I should get.'"

Charlie's reputation brought him the next client, Coleby Hampton who was known as Cole. He was a tall, lean man with large nose. It was a match for his other features that designated strength. His chin protruded and thick eyebrows arched above glasses where his eyes looked out critically upon the world.

Cole was a perfectionist who looked for the best pictures. So far the mountain goat had eluded him and he was told Charlie could change his luck.

The two men walked single file with Charlie leading along high ridges where the view was spectacular. The valley of the Bow River with surrounding, mountainous landscape went unnoticed to Cole who looked only for white patches in high places. Mountain goats with their white fur were as remarkable as the lofty crags where they lived.

Rams had been resting on a ridge above the two men who after a long search stopped. Cole set up his camera and waited.

An eagle screamed. The piercing cry seemed to fit the scene as this bird, frost on its wings, soared past the ledges where goats rested just a little higher than the men.

Cole's camera followed one ram as this majestic part of the mountain stepped to the edge of an overhanging rock. Sunlight shone on curved, black horns, glistened on white fur and brightened the goat's eyes just as this inquisitive monarch first looked into the amber rays then glanced at the lens as picture after picture was snapped to become a once in a lifetime accomplishment. Cole's happiness soared for he knew he had surpassed his dreams. He turned to shout his gratitude to Charlie just as rocks under this famous guide moved.

Charlie swung his arms while attempting to step away from a sliding rock but its momentum increased, throwing him off balance. He turned with one leg stepping into space and arms flailing while he was silhouetted briefly against a backdrop of misty blue then he dropped over the edge and vanished along with tumbling rocks. A rumble of the slide became louder before it settled, swallowed by eerie silence.

Cole could not move. He had been struck first by pure joy then breathtaking loss. Grappling with trying to comprehend what he had just witnessed, he put away his camera then stepped close to the place where Charlie had vanished. Looking over the precipice, the photographer saw only rocks and vast stillness. He returned to the Banff Springs Hotel where he could not stop talking about his trip with the guide, Charlie James.

"The man was the best I've traveled with," stated Cole who was as a haunted person who had seen things he struggled to comprehend and he kept talking in an effort to put into words scenes he could almost not believe of the ram that looked at him, right at the camera as pictures were taken one after the other. Cole developed them and showed everyone he could corner.

"The pictures are the tangible parts of my trip with the guide," he explained. "Much more elusive is any understanding of the sight of Charlie trying to run back toward firm ground as rocks beneath his feet moved out then over a precipice into a roar that was eventually swallowed by a grotesque calm. Even the mountains seemed to become quiet. The goats vanished, remaining only in pictures to prove my account."

Word of Charlie's death reached Isaac Thomas who outfitted a group to return to the base of the rockslide. Tents were set up and fires kindled for searches to begin. Workers always returned without locating Charlie and, at the same time, not wanting to make the discovery.

Cole took pictures of the tent camp. With search attempts always returning without further news, each person knew time was approaching to leave. Searches stopped when night shadows gathered.

Around an evening's fire, Syd Cleever said, "Amazing the impact Charlie James has had on our community in a short time. Seems like he was part of the place and we are all reluctant to let him go."

"We'll never forget him," said Barb Sims who had become uncharacteristically quiet since the tragedy. "I feel like he's still here—and with us."

"What will become of his cabin?" asked Isaac.

"Maybe Barb should have it," offered her father, Fes who had left his work at the mine to help his daughter search. He was a stocky person with unkempt hair, rough beard and dark, blue eyes. "I know the impact he had on her and she always camped at the cabin site."

"The place belongs with Barb," agreed Isaac. The matter seemed settled.

Chapter 4

The Stranger

When Charlie James fell among rocks, a stranger pulled him to safety under a ledge. After the rumbling of the slide subsided, the stranger led Charlie along a path.

"You saved me," whispered Charlie, feeling overwhelming gratitude for another chance at life and appreciating fully the trees, cliffs and sky.

"Happens all the time," replied the man. "People get into trouble then a stranger appears and shows the way to safety."

"I haven't heard of such a thing before," countered Charlie.

"People often don't talk about it, thinking they won't be believed or might be considered to be imagining things. Check the records. The stories are there of a person lost and in a desperate situation until help arrives, showing the way to safety. The accounts are there and can be found if anyone searches. These occurrences take place not only in Banff but all around the world."

"I don't question your help and can't thank you enough for it," declared Charlie.

"Usually the helper appears, shows the way to safety then vanishes," continued the stranger. "This occasion is somewhat different because I was to lead you to safety yet I also want to show you some scenes. We are walking toward the first one now."

At the end of their journey, the stranger pushed aside some foliage before entering what became the entrance to a cave. "I used to come here many times," said the man. "You could start a fire on top of those ashes."

On a section of charred stones and remnant wood, Charlie soon had flames swarming over freshly added kindling then onto larger pieces. Flames moved, sending shadows dancing across walls where in stone there, countless years earlier, had been etched an outline of a great bear.

"I used to come here often with my granddaughter, Raven," said the man. His voice echoed among rock walls and Charlie was caught by such excitement he could only watch and focus on words spoken with a ringing tone as if they represented and held the past.

"My name is Gray Hawk," continued the man. "I am a chief of the Kootenay. Our language, although separate, has a connection to the Algonkian language. Long ago, people who spoke the Algonkian language, particularly the Ojibway, lived to the east beside salt water. Slowly they moved westward, maybe as a result of pressure from Iroquoians who were advancing northward. Moving westward, the Ojibway and other Algonkians pushed against Siouan speaking people such as the Dakotas. The Siouan speakers moved onto the plains—or prairie—and so did Algonkians. People called the Sioux kept somewhat southward and attacked the Kootenay, making us live more in these mountains. Close to us, on the prairie, are the Siouan people, the Stonys. Adjacent Algonkian speakers are the members of the Blackfoot Confederacy along with the more northern Cree.

Today these people live in this area, as does my granddaughter, Raven. I would like you to visit her and remind her again, as I often do, that I watch out for her—and keep in touch."

Standing, Gray Hawk walked to a wall near the bear outline and removed a slab of rock. From the exposed surface, he removed gold nuggets. After dividing them into three equal amounts, he placed each allotment in one of three leather pouches then gave these to Charlie.

"I would like you to keep one of these containers of gold nuggets," he said. "The second I ask you to give to Raven to help her. The third is for Barb. Now I'm going to show you three scenes. Look toward the entranceway."

Charlie glanced toward the cave's mouth and there, as clearly as he had viewed any other event, he saw an assembly of chiefs all wearing traditional attire and he knew immediately they were talking about him. "We like your other abilities too," they said, "but mainly we like your heart."

"Look toward the back of the cave," directed Gray Hawk. Charlie glanced toward the other side and saw a scene he knew was where his cabin was now located. The building was not in this portrayal because the view was of an earlier time and depicted a Kootenay village. Charlie could not believe what he saw next as he recognized himself living with Barb, his wife, and they were Kootenay.

"Yes Charlie," said Gray Hawk. "People don't die. What do you think they do if they have eternal life everyone records in all the religions? People, eternal spirits, come to earth occasionally to experience hard times and develop from such difficulties—always advancing. You and Barb were married and have been at other times. There is no death except for those who choose it by turning away from the Creator."

"How do spirits like Jesus fit into this life?" asked Charlie.

"They are prophets leading people to the Creator," answered Gray Hawk.

"With all the people gathering in traditional attire—is that how people on earth manage to keep their ceremonies, cultures and languages through great difficulties?" asked Charlie.

"Helps to have help," came the reply. "There is constant contact between the spiritual side and earth. When people sleep, they often return home where they will go after a lifetime on earth. I'm a traditional leader but I'm not the only one. I'm the stranger who helped you find safety in a rockslide, but there has been and will be many other strangers—helpers. Just check the records. In the future you will be one of these strangers showing people the way to safety. When you finish your lifetime, you will return to visit earth often as others do."

Chapter 5

The Return

The search had ended. In the morning, the people would return to the village. An extra shot of brew was poured in preparation for sleep when they saw someone approaching. A shadowy figure moved closer. When firelight outlined his features, people gasped.

"Charlie," screamed Barb.

"He is Charlie," declared Fes.

"Where have you been?" asked Syd.

"What happened?" continued Isaac.

"How did you survive that?" asked Cole. "I saw you go down in that slide."

"A stranger pulled me to safety," answered Charlie. "He took me for a walk and we have been talking. I just got back. He said things like this happen all the time—have always been occurring. People will get into desperate situations when a stranger appears, pulls them or shows the way to safety. This time was only different because he introduced himself. Said his name was Gray Hawk. He was Kootenay. He told me about earlier days. Whole thing was fascinating."

"Fascinating," shouted Cole. "I can't believe it but I've seen it. You were carried down by that slide and here you are. You won't believe the fantastic pictures. The majestic ram stepped out on that outcropping in sunlight and looked at the camera when pictures were snapped. The images are achievements of a lifetime and you are unharmed so now I can enjoy the memory and the perfect shots. I have a story to tell that's as incredible as the pictures I can show audiences."

"I'm going to keep you in sight," said Barb. "You can sleep in the tent with my dad and I."

"What a day," proclaimed Syd, as he stood up and started walking to his tent. "What a night."

In the morning, the people returned to their usual work and this brought Charlie back to the welcome sight of his cabin. He kindled a fire in his river stone fireplace and sat back to sip some home brew.

Strange, he mused, *how I got off the train and instead of entering chaos and trouble I've come to what has become this cabin but this building is the smallest part of the home I've found here. I've just found out I've lived here previously, married to the woman I've just met again in these mountains that themselves are filled with life and a spirit tying all of us together. The more we look at one part of life the less we see because all parts are attached, each having a spark of the Creator. I have found peace here. Today I feel it, see it and most surprisingly of all I know I'm part of it.*

The next morning, Charlie was outside cooking breakfast consisting of beans, bannock and coffee when he heard a horse nicker. He looked up and saw two guests arriving.

"Instead of notifying you about your next customer," explained Barb, "I rode out with her because part of her painting trip was to be with horses."

"You both couldn't be more welcome," he replied.

After tying the horses where they could get water and grass, the women approached Charlie, as Barb said, "We brought an extra horse for you to ride. Meet Andrea Stone, an artist and your next client."

"Sit where you are comfortable near the fire and I'll serve breakfast," replied Charlie.

"I like the way he guides people," declared Andrea before she sat down and received the meal starting with coffee. She was tall with a narrow face wrinkled with lines apparently left behind by years of experience and success leaving her with a happy outlook on the world. A distinguishing feature was her grayish-black hair tied at the back into a long braid.

"Charlie, I had no choice but to pick you for a guide," continued Andrea. "You are all they are talking about back at the hotel. Now I can say I have met Charlie James."

"I hope I can match at least part of your expectations," admitted Charlie.

"You already have," she stated. "You've greeted us with hospitality, fine food and a breath-taking view."

"Normal guiding involves a journey," said Charlie. "This excursion can be the same as all the others. There is another possibility however. Usually Barb tells me about a client then I go and see them. This time you have come here. Thereby, you have an extra choice. You could both just stay here. You could paint all day and at night camp here."

"My dreams are fulfilled," she shouted. "I like to ride so I'll ride along the riverbank then paint the water and mountains. Maybe I could get more done in a day than taking time to find a place. Lots of beauty is right here."

"Syd Cleever sent a package for you Charlie," said Barb. She walked to the horses and returned with a bundle she handed him. "Syd provided steaks from his Saloon. He said they are to welcome you back."

"Please thank Syd for me," exclaimed Charlie, receiving the steaks. "They will be for tonight. You can also stay Barb?"

"My cabin renters will have to wait," she replied. "I can't miss this offer."

"I'll be gone most of the day," said Andrea. "As you said, we'll be camping at your cabin tonight and I should leave tomorrow."

"There will be no charge for this guiding journey," he said. "As things have turned out, you're not a client or customer. You're a guest."

"What a wonderful beginning to my painting," she declared. "I've already had a great trip."

After the meal, Andrea prepared to leave for the day, checking her art supplies. "The main task here," she said before leaving, "is not just to find scenes, but to select the best. I would want to include water in paintings anyway so following the river is the best route. By keeping the water in sight, I also know I can't get lost."

"I'll do some riding with Barb," said Charlie, "then we'll come and see your pictures."

"I'd better get working," Andrea stated before nudging her horse and starting to ride along a trail next to the river.

"Barb," said Charlie, "there's something I'd like to show you. We could walk but we can save time by taking the horses."

Charlie led the way along trails. Upon approaching the cave, he suggested tying the horses where they had water and grass. The rest of the route led upward until Charlie said, "In here."

He walked among foliage. Barb followed and was surprised to soon be in a cave where the air smelled of sulfur. Rock ledges surrounded a pool of warm water in a large chamber. In the center were charred remnants of past fires. An outline of a great bear filled much of one wall.

"No one knows about this cavern," whispered Barb as she gazed in awe at the place Charlie had shown her. "Everything about you is amazing, Charlie."

"Gray Hawk brought me here," he explained. "We should respect it as his place and not tell others. Gray Hawk walked to a wall, dislodged an outer layer then pried loose some gold nuggets. He divided them into three equal amounts before placing each allotment into one of three beaded pouches. I was to keep one, give one to his granddaughter, Raven, and give the other to you."

"Why to me I wonder?" she gasped, when Charlie gave her the leather pouch.

"He said he knows you," explained Charlie. "There's a lot more about life than we'll ever discern—or remember. He showed me scenes. One was of the location where I've built my cabin. He presented an impression of a time many years ago when at this same location there was a Kootenay village. You and I were married and lived there. We were Kootenay. Maybe that's why he knows you. In another scene, I saw an assembly of chiefs. Each one was wearing traditional attire. The spirit world, he said, is always with us. We visit back and forth. That's how people get insights and wake up in the morning with solutions to problems. During sleep, we sometimes visit the other side—the spirit world— where there is immortality. We come to earth to experience hard knocks in a process of developing our souls—spirits."

"Thank you, Charlie, for bringing me here," said Barb, "and I must thank Gray Hawk when I can. I know a woman called Raven whose grandfather was Gray Hawk. She comes to Banff to buy supplies."

"Does she live far away?" he asked.

"No," she answered.

"I intended to build a fire here and tell you some of the stories Gray Hawk told me," he explained.

"But we shouldn't be away too long. If you know how to find Raven maybe we should go there now. I have gold to give her."

"I'm really pleased to be part of all these events," whispered Barb.

Looking around at the walls, Charlie said, "According to Gray Hawk, the Kootenay came here for the healing water. They lived more in the mountains when pushed by the Sioux and Blackfoot. There was a time when the Kootenay lived much of the year on the plains although even then the mountains were also home particularly in winter when food was less reliable on the plains but could be located here. Buffalo were present along with sheep, goats, deer, elk and fish. The cabin site and old village place was where fish were caught then dried or smoked along with being enjoyed as a fresh food supply."

Turning and starting to walk toward the cave's entrance, he added, "We should maybe hurry."

Barb rode first. Charlie followed her to a log house with adjacent stable and gardens. Working in the garden, there was a young woman with long, black hair framing her pretty face. She had fine features and dark, brown eyes.

"Hi Barb," said the woman.

"Good morning Shawna," replied Barb. "How is your garden this year?"

"The weeds are winning," she observed. "Good to see you here."

"Is your mother home?" asked Barb.

"Inside," she answered. "Tie your horses at the stable. My brothers are there. They will help you. There's water and hay. I'll tell mother you're here. There is coffee ready."

"Thank you, Shawna," said Barb.

Welcomed at the front door by an older woman with the beauty of a person who saw life as an opportunity, Barb and Charlie were taken to a room where they sat beside a fireplace and received coffee. After thanking Raven, Barb said, "I brought a special person to meet you. He is Charlie James."

Turning to Charlie, Barb added, "This lady is the person you were asked to visit."

"Who asked you to visit," enquired Raven.

"Gray Hawk," he stated.

Her face paling, obviously shocked, Raven placed her cup on a table by her side. She sat back and stared at the fire. Following a long interval, she turned to face Charlie and said, "I want to hear everything."

"I'm a guide," he explained. "I was taking a photographer among high places to photograph goats. While the man was getting the best pictures he had ever seen, I stepped on a slab of rock. It slid and I could not stop the slide. I went over a precipice amid a rockslide. I fell—tumbled but was taken to the shelter of a ledge by a stranger. He took me to a cave where he told me about the Kootenay and showed me a scene of the site where I have built a cabin. But the view he presented to me was of a time long ago when the Kootenay people were camped there. In this village, among the others occupants, there were Barb and I. At that time we too were Kootenay and we were married. Gray Hawk told me about the history of the Kootenay with their allies, the Cree to the north and opponents, the Blackfoot and Sioux—including Stonys who are Sioux.

Gray Hawk says he watches over you and sends you signs of his presence. Spiritual people from the other side visit those presently undertaking the human experience. Such contact occurs all the time although the spirits usually go unnoticed. As I mentioned, Gray Hawk sends you signs. I'm intended to be one of them. Also he sends help. He walked to one of the cave's walls. Beside an outline of a great bear, he dislodged gold nuggets. He divided them into three equal amounts then placed each allotment into one of three beaded, leather pouches. I received one and was told to give one to Barb. He knows Barb from the past. I was instructed to bring one of these three pouches to you and here it is."

Charlie stood up and took Raven the leather bag. She received it, saying "Thank you."

She held it and otherwise did not move. Charlie sat, sipped the drink and waited.

"I know who you are," she said, speaking softly yet her words carried clearly as there were no competing background intrusions except for snapping sounds occasionally coming from burning wood in the fireplace. "You built your cabin at a site our family has used as a camping place for generations— in the winter. There was more food in the mountains than on the unpredictable prairie where we used to live so much of the time during other seasons. Your cabin site is on our traditional fishing place. Your visit I will long cherish. Barb, I am equally pleased to see you."

"When you get a chance we will look forward to your visit at the cabin that is your traditional fishing place," said Charlie. "Hopefully we are not intruding as we previously lived there likely with you."

"Yes," she replied. "And you're not intruding. Will you stay for a meal?"

"Thank you, but we must check on a guest who is now at the cabin," he replied. "She is an artist and busy for the day painting."

"I'm pleased she isn't a hunter," said Raven. "Kootenay have been hunters but they hunted for food when there were many animals and comparatively few hunters. More tourist hunters are coming here all the time and almost all of them don't hunt because they need food. Saying they use the food is insulting because using food only occurs because the meat is there so it might as well be cooked—likely is enjoyed. The essential aspect is that such food is not needed—required for life. The priority for tourist hunters is the kill. This is a sacrilege. Trophy hunting is the worst form of disrespect. Today there are less and less animals all the time with always more hunters. This won't end well. The slaughter of the buffalo was a tragedy and left many Indian people without food. Wildlife must be respected and tourist hunters should only hunt on ranches. The same is true for trappers who don't actually need the money. Using money is not the same as needing it. Trappers, too, can get their money from fur farms, which is also true about trees. Fortunately tourists can't shoot these mountains for sport. Wild life, like the mountains, should be respected and shot only by photographers and painters. Most of all wild life is to resonate with our souls and brings us in touch with the Creator."

"This is a visit I'll remember," whispered Barb.

"It'll be remembered and often spoken of," added Raven. "This is another sign from Gray Hawk."

"Your last name is Gray Hawk?" asked Charlie.

"Yes," she said. "That name means a lot to me."

"I can certainly see why," said Barb.

"We should not neglect our guest back at the cabin," noted Charlie. "Thank you for your hospitality."

"I appreciate everything about your visit," replied Raven.

Barb and Charlie rode back. At the cabin, Barb said, "I'll follow the river trail and see how Andrea has been getting along with her painting."

"Good idea," noted Charlie. "When you return I'll have Syd's steaks ready."

Sunlight was deepening with red hues along with first shadows of evening when the two women rode into the clearing where Charlie was preparing to add steaks to skewers above the flames.

"I'm enjoying the most outstanding trip I've ever had," exclaimed Andrea after the horses had been looked after for the night. "They said at the hotel Charlie was the best and I'd be lucky if I got him. The stories I thought must be just rumors. My time with you folks though is beyond my highest hopes or expectations. Now steaks are being cooked over the fire. You don't use a frying pan Charlie?"

"Not with steaks," he answered. "Pans cause searing and toughen the meat. Tenderness remains when heat is applied directly to the steaks. For our meal, there are also fried potatoes. Syd included apple pie."

After sitting on a chair next to Barb, Andrea explained, "Usually I'm quite distant, reserved, with people, especially those I've just met. During this journey, however, I'm able to relax with friends.

Usually I take a long time before accepting a person as a friend. Here I'm with friends."

"We react the same way to you," observed Barb. "Being a person who works all the time, as you also seem to be, I appreciate having Charlie prepare the meal."

"So do I," noted Andrea.

"Barb's father makes the drinks," explained Charlie, as he gave each woman a glass of home brew. He stopped to take a sip from a third glass before declaring, "Steaks are ready."

He served the food on rounded boards, or platters, he had made for meals. Knives and forks accompanied each board. The usual salt and pepper were also passed around.

"Never have enjoyed a more tender and delicious steak," exclaimed Andrea. "You're certainly right about the pans. Do you skewer other foods?"

"Anything firm enough to not break apart," he answered. "Trout cook well and quickly."

"What a meal," whispered Andrea while she looked around at the deepening colors of night's approach, the comparatively brightening fire and two companions who had become her friends.

"Your paintings caught the colors that are unique to this landscape," observed Barb. "The bluish or turquoise hues in water come from glaciers."

"There are varying shades of blue in forested slopes," added Charlie.

"And the sky of course is constantly changing," said Andrea. "If I wasn't getting so tired, I'd like to paint this scene around the fire. I'll probably be able to do pictures from memory. All scenes will not be complete because there are no colors to represent friendship."

Talk continued while the moon first appeared in reddish-orange light that drained away as the sphere moved higher until there was only a silver sheen covering forested slopes and the river's surface.

"I regret the need for sleep," said Andrea, softly. "I'm in a spell of such colors and magnificence; I think this might lead to a matching dream. I'll go and see." She finished the home brew in her glass then walked into the cabin, leaving Barb and Charlie beside the fire.

"I'm enjoying this time so much I don't need more but I feel brave, or unrestricted, enough to see what more would be like," declared Barb. "I'm going to continue what you started the last time."

She walked toward Charlie who met her. They enjoyed each other's company through the night.

In the morning when surrounding scenery brightened with the dawn, they both prepared the first meal of the day inside the cabin. Awakening, Andrea heard sounds of people talking and also noted a tantalizing aroma of perking coffee. She walked into the kitchen, finding a place set for her along with a table topped by fried potatoes, beans and flapjacks.

"The best of all times continues," she whispered after sitting down on a chair across from Barb and Charlie. "You have prepared another wonderful meal. Did either of you sleep at all last night?"

"No," said Barb.

"No," added Charlie.

"How many times does a woman have to come here before getting a no sleep night?" Andrea asked, smiling.

"At least one lifetime," answered Barb.

Chapter 6

Dark Sky

Charlie continued guiding. A waiting list of people requesting him was of such length he was as busy as he wanted to be. For supplies, he used some gold from the pouch given to him by Gray Hawk.

Returning from another successful guiding excursion, he was a contented man. He was making plans for the future with Barb and his dreams had come to the present where he walked today pleased with the way things were to such an extent he no longer lived in the future for the someday. He felt all he wanted was being accomplished. However, today, while walking back to his cabin, a cloud seemed to have drifted across his clear sky. For the moment he was caught by a sense of foreboding. Like cold mist coming down from high country, he had a premonition of trouble coming or present. He tried to shake off the notion but he could not leave it behind. It kept staying ahead, adding a gray film in front of his view of trees and distant peaks. Sunshine lacked its usual warmth and did not dispel the grayness.

Approaching his cabin, he halted. *The area seems to be as expected,* he thought. I'm just imagining things. *Everything will be all right.* He proceeded onward. Close to the front door, he stopped after hearing behind him a sound that was out of place as if something or someone had stepped on and snapped a twig.

A blast filled everything he knew before pain took over the sound. There was another sharp report then only bright light where he saw his parents. They waited for him and he walked to them, while being greeted by a dog that had been his friend back at the family farm.

"Let's go," shouted Reg to his other two accomplices. "Someone might've heard the shots. He led Len and Case to the cabin, went inside and they started searching. "He has been paying with gold nuggets," continued Reg. "They'll be hidden in some unlikely place."

Finding the pouch in a space behind a picture, they rushed back to their horses. The three men rod away along a route they had intended to take. It removed them from the killing and brought them to a distant valley containing a cabin they wanted.

In Banff, Barb felt an unease that extra work would not dispel. When she heard that Charlie had not shown up for one of his scheduled guiding adventures, she could not put off acting on her worry any longer. Her father was home at the time. She told him she was going to see if anything had happened to Charlie.

"You're not the worrying kind," said Fes. "If you're concerned, I should go with you this time."

"Your company I would welcome," she replied.

They rode quietly to the cabin. Stricken with grief, Barb stared. Not accepting what she saw.

Fes completed the necessary work behind the cabin. Later they would put up a marker.

"It was a robbery," he told Barb during the ride back to Banff. "Inside they tore the place apart looking for money—or gold."

"They would've heard about his gold," whispered Barb. "I know who I suspect."

"We suspect the same three," he replied. "I'll notify the police."

Days passed although time remained still for Barb who could not get beyond the tragedy. She kept busy although nothing helped.

One of the people who came to rent a cabin awakened something inside her when he paid with gold.

"You planning to stay a long time?" she asked, looking at him more carefully. He had shoulder length gray hair with a similar growth of beard. Visible remnants of his face were lined and well-tanned. Watery blue eyes sparkled when he said, "I plan to be a while. I need a cabin until I build a new place here in Banff. I've long planned to move into the community where I'd get to talk to people more often. When a chance came to make the move, I agreed to it. Got a good price for my home in the mountains. Guys paid with gold. They're a shifty lot. Always smirkin' or grinnin' back and forth, as if sending messages I wouldn't like if I heard them. The three men were too sneaky to come right out with anything. I got well paid so I left. I can now rebuild. I'm Howard Ridge—prospector most o' the time but didn't find much until those three showed up."

That's the proof I've waited for, thought Barb. *Reg, Len and Case aren't successful at anything, including prospecting. They have Charlie's gold. Dad is at the mine. Cabins are fine. I'll carry out my plan.*

Banff

After sliding her rifle into its case at the pinto's side along with positioning two pistols in holsters secured to her belt, Barb left at first light. She followed trails connecting a route Howard had mentioned for the location of the cabin he had sold.

I feel steeled by conviction I have to do what I'm planning, she resolved to herself. *I'm not just looking for revenge. I think there is essential justice and all of it is violated, leaving me unable to rest, knowing those men are sneering, grinning back and forth with each other, sharing behind the back of the rest of the world their secret and great victory. They were, after all these years of being looked down on, now successful. They have a home, money for supplies; and could be taken as men who stopped being constant failures.*

Of all the scenes the three men might have expected to see during an average day, the last possibility imaginable was what they now saw in the increasingly obvious form of Barb Sims riding toward their cabin.

"I'll approach holding the rifle in case she is some king o' trouble," said Reg to Len and Case before he motioned one man to circle to the left and the other to the right. After the other two men had gone out the back, Reg opened the front door. Carrying his rifle, he stepped outside to talk to the rider.

"Why would you come here?" he asked.

"I'm here because the three of you killed Charlie James," she stated. As she spoke, her right hand gripped her rifle case. Leaving the weapon in its place, she reached in, moved the front of the leather sleeve upward then she pulled the trigger. The blast knocked Reg over sending him sprawling onto his back. Her shocked pony sidestepped, moving Barb away as a bullet passed the side of her face. Removing a pistol from its holster, she turned, saw the form behind her and fired. Len shot once into the ground then fell forward. Hearing the third man rustling bushes to one side, Barb saw his outline and spurred her horse forward, charging directly while shooting. Case stood, stared blankly then fell into a tangle of brush.

Barb rode away from the cabin, dismounted and walked back to erase tracks along with any other sign of her presence. Lastly she adjusted the area slightly to easily fit an interpretation that the killers had argued among themselves and shot each other. With completed scene depicting a self-inflicted shootout, Barb rode away thinking, at last I feel freed from a burden that has darkened the sky for me since the murder of Charlie James.

Chapter 7

The Visitor

When cabins started to be rented more on a long-term basis, Barb had extra time to help Isaac Thomas with his outfitting business.

"I'm busier all the time," said Isaac to Barb at the start of one excursion with hunters. "I appreciate your help not only for your medical experience but also you can do other chores on the trail including packing, horse handling and cooking, not to mention guiding. I don't have to worry about you getting lost.

After Isaac stepped up into the saddle, Barb replied, "I enjoy your trips, although this group is hunting. I don't like helping them."

"You're helping me," he explained. "And I appreciate it. I don't like hunting either; but right now it's part of the business. It's going on with or without us. Someday it'll end. Until then, we have a chance to present our side."

"OK Isaac," she concluded. "I'm pleased to help you."

"Thank you," he replied. "I think we're ready to leave."

The pack train started winding single file along a trail used many times. Branches to the main route provided variety farther away from the ranch. Air was cool, sky was clear, opening a morning promising to bring another day when first rays of sunlight shone on mountain peaks and brought to life parts of the forest that rest at night.

While the landscape was a place of unlimited variety the pack train added comfort of uniformity with each horse always walking in the same place in the line. *Riding on the trail*, mused Barb, while the line of horses moved slowly onward, *is much like sitting on a chair at home. I can rest and have time to wonder if I should ever again agree to take hunters into my wilderness to kill something and take it away.*

At camp in the evening with tents pitched and meal finished, Barb sat with the others around the fire. *Generally, campfire talk*, reflected Barb, *is a time of the excursion that I look forward to when there is a summing up of the day and plans are made for events to come in a journey that turns to reality what has for so long, sometimes even a lifetime, been only a dream. With other groups, conversation settles around a perfect picture snapped or a unique painting done in special light to stir for endless day's memories of happiest times. On a hunting trip, talk too often centers not just on magnificent wildlife but killing it.*

"Making a perfect shot and getting a trophy animal is a thrill beyond description," said Carl, one of the hunters. As with the others, his clothing and guns represented the best available in outdoor stores. Although now, in the wilderness, he continued established routines of having his gray hair well combed and somewhat plain face washed. Braced by evening drinks, he became talkative. "Only those who have been there can really know this type of excitement," he continued. "There's the feeling our pioneers had of bringing home food to the family. Now this feeling goes to getting a good kill or another trophy for my wall—a head with fine horns, a hide or meat."

"Pioneers hunted because the birds or animals were not just used but actually needed for food," stated Barb. "Also wildlife was numerous but game has been getting scarce and there are more hunters all the time. Buffalo have almost disappeared from the plains. We presently have to cherish wildlife while they enjoy their own lives. Today we have to produce food or furs on farms and let remaining wildlife live. We can enjoy being in these mountains not just in getting something shot."

"You don't understand," replied Carl.

"You haven't changed," observed Barb. "You just don't see that wildlife has changed. There are less of them now and more hunters. We have to protect what remains before it is lost. The whole wilderness web of life is a system in harmony where even animal predators have a place in removing sickness, although such work might seem imperfect to us. Predators, such as wolves can smell—be aware of—sickness, get attracted to it and use this as a food source. There's a purpose for everything and each part is in balance. People can belong if they recognize they are outside, external predators who are there not to remove illness but to kill the best and healthiest of wildlife. People can be accepted if they stop being external predators and be part of the system as a photographer, painter, adventurer or naturalist. Wildlife has awareness of such people and accepts them, although recognition often takes time. Hunters did not throw the system out of balance until they became too numerous and numbers of wildlife lessened—even became scarce. We must cherish what is left before it is lost like the buffalo—with disastrous results."

To Isaac, Carl asked, "Are you sure this person should be taking out a group of hunters?"

"I don't know what I'd do without her," he answered. "She's a packer, naturalist, guide, gun expert and horse handler. She can run the outfit and look after a camp. I appreciate her contribution particularly as cook and above all as doctor. She looks after injuries in Banff. If someone shoots you and cuts off your head to put it on a wall as a trophy, she could sew your head back on again."

"What side are you on here?" inquired Carl.

"I enjoy life in these mountains," he said. "I'm like the people I've seen holler with pure joy of being in such grandeur. I share the experience. I'm lucky to get paid for doing what I want to do."

The next day, the group came to a remote, well-forested area where there was a variety of wildlife although not many of them, making the hunt challenging. Hunters spread out, each one going after different game. One wanted a grizzly while others sought a sheep, goat, mule deer or elk.

To the camp that evening, the hunters had returned except for one. A successful hunter skinned a grizzly while another person worked on a ram with trophy horns. A mule deer had also been shot. Steaks were the main part of the evening's meal. One man,

George Carson, was late returning. He was an almost overweight person who saw a hunting trip as a chance to keep the weight down. He was somewhat non-descript except for a waxed moustache and light blue eyes.

George had shot a deer. Although he had gutted it, the remainder was too heavy to carry so he started dragging it. To reduce the struggle, he took a short cut back to camp. A route that was supposed to save time turned out to be longer. When darkness started to settle in around him he tried to walk faster. Regardless of an attempt to hurry, one section of densely treed terrain just led to another. He fought panic. He was sweating and breathing heavily when the stranger appeared.

"You should rest," said the stranger.

Comforted by having company with the added likelihood this person could help him get back to camp, George stopped and almost cried with relief. "You're a welcomes sight," he whispered just as he realized he was wet with sweat.

"I'll show you the way to your camp," said the man.

"You have saved me," exclaimed George after they both sat down.

With surprising speed, the stranger started a small fire sending light flickering across the adjacent area. An owl hooted. George welcomed the calls because the forest appeared friendly again and in its own way was speaking.

"You're as welcome to me as any friend I've ever met," said George. "From now on I'm going to enjoy owls because they too gave me company when I never felt so alone. I had started to see the wilderness as an enemy."

"You treat it as an enemy," said the man. "You have always treated it as an enemy. You even shoot it."

"I like to pit my skills against the challenge of being out here," he explained. "Finding animals is hard work. Even the slightest shift in air currents can take my scent to the target. There is great difficulty in getting close enough to an animal to get a good shot. Not just the killing brings me out on these adventures. There's the camaraderie, tenting, campfire cooking—the traveling. A whole package of interests brings me hunting year after year."

"How important is the killing?" asked the man.

"It's just part of the package," he answered.

"Just one aspect of the whole experience?" enquired the stranger again.

"Yes," said George. "Just one part."

"Would you come without the killing?" asked the man.

Although he was sweating, George suddenly felt cold and he shook with the chill. He saw the deer, then this man sitting on the other side of a small, flickering flame. George could not reply because he knew the answer and could not say it.

"I will show you where your camp is located," said the stranger before he snuffed out the fire. When he was certain it was extinguished, he started to walk through the woods. Dragging the deer, George followed. In a short time, he asked the man, "Could we stop? I have a question."

The man turned and George said, "Isn't it unusual that you should just appear and show me the way to go back?"

"Happens all the time—through the ages," he answered. "People get lost—caught in desperate situations. A stranger arrives and shows the way to safety. These occasions have happened at Banff many times and will again."

The man continued walking until the camp came into view. Seeing the light of the fire with people around, George was overjoyed. He turned to express his gratitude but his helper had vanished.

When George stepped into light cast by the fire, there were gasps of relief and more than one person asked, "What happened to you?"

"What happened to me?" repeated George, as he sat down. He was given a well—spiked drink before he said again, "What happened to me? I'm still trying to figure that out myself; but I can tell you many things happened to me. I shot a deer. I gutted it. It was heavy so I dragged it. I took what I thought was a short cut back to camp and got lost. I was starting to fight panic when a stranger appeared. What a welcome sight. He said I should rest. We sat down and between us he quickly prepared a small fire. Its light brightened our area as night had arrived. An owl hooted. I've heard them before but I'll listen to them more in the future for the call was additional company for me—as if the forest was speaking—and I told the man I had started to feel the forest was an enemy. The man said that I was treating it as an enemy. I was shooting it.

The shooting is only one part of the whole trip, I replied. Then he asked me if I would come without the kill.

I know the answer to that question and I'll never hunt again.

I asked him if it was unusual for me to meet a stranger who appeared just at the right time and showed me the way back to camp. He said this happens all the time and I should just check the records. So that's what happened to me and I'm still thinking about the whole amazing experience."

"Did the stranger tell you his name?" asked Barb Sims.

"Yes," George answered. "He said he was Charlie James."

Chapter 8

The Painter

The next person to be taken out on horseback was a repeat visitor, Andrea Stone. This time she brought other members of her art club.

Paint boards, canvases, brushes, paints, easels and other artistic equipment were added to the usual supplies packed on horses. In single file, each horse had the same place in line with some having riders while other horses carried packs. The guests marveled at the special colors of the land of extremes where snow-capped peaks rose above slowly drifting clouds. Valleys were expansive and cut by wide, pebble-bottomed rivers joined occasionally by streams rushing between narrow banks or cascading down rock walls. Eagles sometimes soared overhead while mule deer were silhouetted against backgrounds of green meadows.

After a camp was established, each artist selected a site with a scene to be painted. While Andrea filled a canvas with broad strokes of color to get the first picture started, Barb brought her a cup of coffee before sitting down to enjoy the company of this friend.

"Sorry about Charlie," said Andrea. "After such an incredible visit I enjoyed with you the last time, I had to return. I've been telling these other artists about the best painting experience I've ever encountered so this time they wanted to be included. I tried to get Charlie again as a guide and was given the news. They said you were outfitting with Isaac. Therefore, I signed up along with the art club."

"More tourists are coming to Banff all the time," observed Barb. "I get called more often to help with outfitting. The cabin rental business also gets busier. My dad is building more cabins. He helps with the renting because I'm often assisting Isaac. People agreed that I should have Charlie's cabin but I couldn't go back. I gave it to my father. He lives there now and has left the mine. He's completely occupied by the cabin business."

"My friends are enjoying their adventure," noted Andrea. "We meet for painting excursions although they're finding this trip to be the best of them."

"You couldn't be in a better place for scenery," observed Barb.

"Or for stories," added Andrea. "I liked seeing you and Charlie together. You had such a connection it fit with the incredible presence and lofty grandeur of these mountains. Banff is a place where everything is spectacular, akin to what there was between you and Charlie. Did they ever find the people who shot him?"

"Three known thieves started spending gold they didn't find themselves because they weren't prospecting," she answered. They used gold to buy a cabin from Howard Ridge who rented a cabin from me while he built his new residence in Banff. He told me the three men had used gold to buy his cabin. The facts are they had stolen the gold from Charlie. That's why they shot him. The three thieves were themselves shot in a shootout at their cabin. The police say there must've been an argument and the thieves shot each other."

"Justice stalks these mountains," stated Andrea, looking directly at Barb's eyes and seeing, in the depths of blue, the spirit there had been between her and Charlie and a match for these mountains. "My friends are starting to paint what they see in the landscape," continued Andrea. "I hope they become aware, as I have, of the people who have a transcending spirit connecting with the scenery including wildlife, rivers, valleys, forests and snow-capped peaks rising above the clouds."

"You can paint with words too," whispered Barb. "I enjoy your pictures."

"I enjoy your company," added Andrea before she started checking her painting supplies. "That's why I came here."

The artists got busy sorting equipment. The camp soon became quiet after artists walked away to select from unlimited possibilities the special topic to be preserved in a picture.

The sun moved across a vast sky. Gradually colors of evening gathered and deepened before shadows started to bring people back to sit around a central fire in camp. A wide selection of foods had been prepared along with Barb's specialty of skewered beefsteaks. She also had two other favorite preparations of roasted trout along with fried or baked bannock. Tea and coffee were almost always available. With evening shadows darkening to bring the night, Barb offered home brew either separately or as an addition to other drinks. Each outfitting excursion included pies baked at Syd Cleever's saloon.

One artist, Bonnie Angus, was late returning, causing some worry to circulate at the camp. Night settled in, making the fire seem brighter. Firelight flickered across surrounding rocks and trees.

When despair was at its peak, the form of Bonnie stepped into the firelight. She was a slim woman with white hair protruding from a leather cap. A well-tanned face revealed an outdoor lifestyle. Her dark eyes completed her striking appearance. A cheer went up as she was welcomed back. She sat down and enjoyed all the attention as one delicious food item after another was brought to her.

Following the meal and a shot of brew, Andrea said, "OK Bonnie, what happened?"

"I was painting and did not notice the time until I lost sufficient light to work on my picture," she explained. "I was shocked by how the night was upon me. I rushed to put away my paints and store the masterpiece. Worried by the darkness, I hurried along what I thought was the right way until I knew I was in trouble. Panicking, I started walking faster when a stranger appeared and said, "Your camp is this way."

I followed him. Nothing has looked better than the sight of your fire. I turned to thank him and he had gone."

"Did you get his name?" asked Barb.

"No," she replied. "And I'm sorry I didn't get to thank him for saving me.

Chapter 9

The Holiday

Banff kept attracting more tourists, increasing work with cabin rentals and outfitting. In spite of having extra requests for her help, Barb started taking holidays. She stored cooking and camping supplies in packs tied on her horse. Well provisioned, she rode up into high places, selecting favorite locations for a lean-to and fire where there was also water and grass for the pinto.

Having set up a comfortable camp and with her horse well positioned, Barb walked to the adjacent stream to set out a line. She fished until catching one or two trout before returning to spit or pan-fry the fish.

These occasions, with the company of mountains, restored to her restfulness she had not felt since Charlie had been shot. *I enjoy the company of people*, she mused after two trout had been placed in a pan where oil sizzled. *These rock edifices also have presence with their loftiness and all the life attracted to them. Eagles nest in the highest crags. There are more birds and animals along with trees on lower slopes. Only goats appear on high ledges. Sometimes sheep venture where ravens fly. There is life here and I feel this companionship. I'm told I'm alone too much; yet I think I've never been alone. I enjoy silence as it brings depth of rest. We know the lack of noise as silence, however, there is no total absence of sound. I can hear this silence. In it, there is the presence of spirit along with a far off murmur of rushing water or a blend of voices from animals and birds mixed with a whisper of wind. Into this background, there occasionally comes a piercing cry of a hawk or nightly hooting of an owl. I like to hear the owls the most. They are the voice of the forest. The dark realm of a forest at night is hidden from the view of people but is the time of most activity for wildlife. The owls see all of the forest and express it in their calls.*

Drawn away from her thoughts by an awareness of a presence, Barb looked up from the frying pan.

After her eyes adjusted to darkness beyond the flames, she saw the form of a person, standing, watching her.

"Oh Charlie," screamed Barb. "I knew you'd come."

He approached and she asked, "Can I hold you?"

"I'm a spirit," he answered. "We're already as close as two people can get."

He sat down beside the fire and Barb asked, "Would you have a trout?"

"No, thank you," he answered.

"Would you like some brew?" she inquired after putting aside the pan and bringing out a bottle.

"OK," he replied. She filled one cup then reached for a second.

"I have to have a shot—to celebrate," she said. "I keep taking these holidays when I don't have time for them and now you—at last—are here."

"I've always been here," he said. "On the other side, in the spirit world, we can be in more than one place at once."

"This is one of the places I've been calling you for a long time," she stated after giving him a full cup.

"Thank you," he said. "We don't need food or liquid but this is a treat I'll share with you like this visit."

"You should never have left me," she stated.

"I didn't," he said. "Now, you just can't see me."

"You know what I mean," she countered. "You should not have got shot."

"Sorry," he said, smiling. "It was difficult to avoid bullets coming from the back."

"That's how Reg, Len and Case fight," she stated.

"Yes," he agreed. "Not how they died though," he added, smiling. "They saw who shot them and so did I. Thank you. I knew their days were numbered. Spirits such as those who have turned away from God don't come back to the sacred other side or heaven. These turned away spirits keep getting sent into new births and eventually will be part of earth mass. They do this to themselves by turning away from God. There are prophets like Jesus and others, including Handsome Lake who show people the way home. Each person can decide to come home on his or her own. We come to earth to learn and develop from hard times that don't exist in the spiritual side. We come to earth sometimes often in different lifetimes. You and I were once camped at the cabin site. Then we were Kootenay and we were married."

"I wanted us to get married this time too," she declared.

"I did too," he said.

"Why didn't you ask me?" she inquired.

"I got shot," he said.

"Before that," she continued.

"I waited until I was sure I wouldn't get rejected," he confessed.

"You should've known," she stated.

"Never assume what I know about women and one I love," he confirmed.

"I hope I remember that if we get a second chance to come back as people," she said.

"Please do—or I'll remind you," he noted.

"Will we get another chance Charlie?" she asked.

"When we are at home in the spirit world we decide what we want to develop in our spirits for each experience on earth," he explained. "We'll have another chance."

"Now I have hope and I can resume my life here," she declared.

"That's why I came," he explained.

"Thank you—more brew?" she asked.

"OK," he replied.

"Will the rest of my life here be happy?" she asked.

"We don't get to see our futures because we come here to experience and we won't learn if we know the story before it starts. I know your story. We see it all when we get home to the spiritual side where we live. I can tell you though you will generally be happy and have a successful lifetime."

"You have given me the contentment I have lacked since you went away," she confirmed. "I'll always be grateful for this visit."

"On the spiritual side there is no sense of time," he noted. "You will come to see me almost immediately. Your time here on earth though will seem longer. You will have a long wait. I won't."

"You've given me rest, Charlie," she observed. "You've given me hope."

Charlie finished the brew, as did Barb. When she put down her glass and looked for Charlie, he had gone.

He has left, Barb said to herself. *But I'll always feel now that he is with me and I can stop taking holidays. I don't need them anymore.*

Chapter 10

Present Day

As Clara Elder and Sethrum James drove along another road in Banff, Clara said, "If these mountains could talk, imagine the stories they could tell. One of those accounts I want to write and I talked you into coming with me during this journey in a search or quest for my story.

Seth's hair and beard, having been black, now had a tinge of gray, showing his years of experience as a tourist guide. His facial features revealed strength although most noticeable were his black eyes indicating depth in his view of life.

Clara was beautiful although she treated it casually, letting blondish hair tumble with little restriction around her face where brown eyes sparkled. Her recently acquired position of associate history professor enabled her to impart to others the past not as an end of a journey but as a segment portraying the future.

"With all the records of people in the past at Banff," she continued, "I'm looking for one story standing out from all the others to catch my attention."

"What information have you gathered so far?" enquired Seth.

"Glad you asked," she exclaimed with her eyes sparkling. "Everything begins with the earliest historians, those who keep legends among the first people who lived here for thousands of years. Many nations met in the present day Bow River Valley of Banff. They met to celebrate life with social events including dancing, singing and storytelling around evening fires. Trading took place. And of course there was competition for influence and power. Among mountain people there were the Kootenay who during earlier days lived much of the time on the prairie. They moved more into the high country because of the advance of others such as the Algonkian speaking Blackfoot along with Siouan Stoney. The Cree moving into the north were allies. These original groups are represented today during a celebration of traditions known as Banff Indian Days. Here the start of this region's story can be heard and seen.

"The latest part of Banff's record starts with the arrival of Europeans who, along with the foundation of the first nations, established the United States to the south and Canada in the north. To tie Canada together there came the Canadian Pacific Railway. The first nations living here saw economic opportunity in tourists arriving by train. The Indigenous people also welcomed law and order maintained by the Royal Canadian Mounted Police. Banff started in 1883 as Railway Siding 29, renamed Banff from Banffshire, in Scotland, the birthplace of Canadian Pacific Railway President George Stephen. In 1885, the Federal Government established the Banff Hot Springs Reserve to protect the hot springs. Two years later, the area was expanded with the forming of Rocky Mountains Park Reserve, a joint venture of the Federal Government and the Canadian Pacific Railway. The railway built hotels mainly Banff Springs and Chateau Lake Louise. In 1930, the National Parks Act changed the name Rocky Mountains Park to Banff National Park. By this time most visitors were arriving by car.

"These are just a few facts for an article I'd like to write about Banff," explained Clara. "The real story is inside the facts, beyond the surface layer of dates and actions of a few people. If only the mountains could talk—they would tell stories greater than our wildest hopes or dreams. Yet by gathering surface details we start to hear the mountains speaking. We just haven't been listening."

"A grizzly," exclaimed Seth. "He's coming directly at us." Seth swerved off the pavement and parked on the side of the road. Passing in front of the car, the bear jumped down an embankment and stopped to eat grasses.

Putting down her side window, Clara said, "I can get pictures."

"I'm going to get out to take some," replied Seth before opening his door and stepping outside. He was watching the feeding bear when he heard a deep growl. Turning, he saw the massive form of a second bear following the first. Facing the jaws and teeth, Seth slowly backed out of the giant's path and the bear agilely continued down the embankment. After eating some grasses, both grizzlies moved out of sight beyond brush.

Relaxing, Seth got back into the car where Clara said, "That was close."

"Those bears look large at a distance," he whispered. "Up close, they seem like a furred chunk of a mountain. Maybe we could try something more relaxing and drive down to Icefields Parkway, Highway 93."

"We could go to the Crossing Resort," added Clara.

"Good idea," agreed Seth.

They stopped at the resort, got a room then went to the restaurant for an evening meal. After sitting at a table where Clara got wine and Seth received beer, they both ordered Arctic char.

"A lot easier than having to catch and cook it ourselves," said Clara before enjoying some wine. "When David Thompson came through here in 1810, he didn't get this service. At that time, there was a need for food and wildlife, although in decline, could provide for the needs of a small number of people. Some buffalo remained here when Thompson's group traveled through this area. Now buffalo have gone."

When the meals arrived, Seth said, "Char is the finest fish. It's also farmed."

"Certainly delicious," agreed Clara. "Tomorrow, we could get a take-out coffee and have breakfast at Chateau Lake Louise."

"Yes," he replied. "Between here and there the scenery is spectacular."

The next morning, following a breakfast upholding the Chateau Lake Louise's reputation for finest meals, Clara and Seth signed up for a trip with an outfitter. Driving to the ranch, they turned onto a driveway and the ranch emerged from behind trees.

Soon after arriving, the two travelers were on horseback in a line of other riders following a trail bordered by forested slopes. The group stopped at an established site located beside a cliff where a stream left the top of a rock wall and fell in lacey tendrils splashing down to a pool. It provided cold, clear water for horses and people. Fires were started and the camp cook was preparing a meal consisting of buffalo burgers and beefsteaks, all purchased from area ranches.

"You're living up to your reputation," said Clara to the group leader, Sara Thomas, a woman raised to breed and train riding horses. Blonde hair protruded from under a well-worn Stetson.

Sara's dark blue eyes flashed as she explained, "Other members of the family are mainly leaving the ranch now. They are looking for a change. This place has been in the family for generations and was started by one of Banff's first outfitters, Isaac Thomas. He built the place out of logs. The woman who helped on trail rides was Barb Sims. They were married and had two children, a boy and a girl. The camp leaders today are all related to these founders. Barb Sims started the method of skewering steaks over the fire. Oil drips right into the flames, providing one less attraction to bears. After meals, greasy pans don't have to be washed. They sear and toughen the meat. Meat for buffalo burgers comes from ranches now just like beef. Today we have to produce our food."

"When we were selecting an outfitter for this ride," continued Seth, as they sat beside the fire, "we were told you served the best meals and had been in business since Banff started to be called Banff."

"Yes," said Sara. "We've been here since the beginning and this is my life."

"You couldn't choose a better one," agreed Clara. "You must like horses."

"I do," she stated. "They're all individuals and I enjoy getting to know them. They become friends. Many people use animals just for what they can do and overlook the best of them—their individuality—their spirits. They are different from us but important in their own lives. We can share our common connection we have together, as with all life, and here we are elevated to the kernel, the sacredness of life and not just the chaff. Some people hit dogs or horses along with people and miss the joy of life I experience riding out here. Occasionally, my horse will look toward a shallow, pebbly river and nicker. I stop, take off the saddle and away she goes to roll in the water. That's what I mean by a horse being a friend. Sometimes I take off my clothes and go for a swim too. That's why I say this is my life."

"You're a successful person," declared Seth. "I'm pleased Clara and I came on this trail ride."

"I'm glad you did too," added Sara before walking away to sort equipment following the meal.

"I feel as if we've met something out here," said Clara. "We heard the mountains telling us another of the stories if we are listening to hear them. Strands of life wind together and we can hear the mountains speak—one strand at a time."

"I feel uplifted—a sense of elation—after going on that trail ride," explained Seth while the two travelers drove to the isolated cabin they had rented.

"I have that same awareness," replied Clara. "Almost a feeling of coming home."

"That's it," he declared. "Sometimes we seem to fight life and everything we attempt is blocked by one obstacle after another. Then there are journeys such as the one unfolding before us where each part seems to light our way to the next."

"The story of Banff is unfolding before us," said Clara. "You and I are experiencing revelations and I'm not going to hide our findings in a report read only by other historians. I'm going to write an account for a journal or magazine to share widely with others what we are discovering."

"You have a good purpose in wanting to share what we find," he stated.

"Our discoveries should be shared," continued Clara. "There is no such thing as separateness in life. It's all connected and we should proceed accordingly."

"We have arrived," declared Seth as he stopped the car in front of a path winding among trees toward a partially visible log cabin. "Here we should stay for a few days."

"Certainly this is a place where we could stop for hopefully a long time," agreed Clara.

"Let's unload as we look around," said Seth.

They entered the building through a side door and stepped into a kitchen. It shone with cleanliness. There were two bedrooms, one on each side of the kitchen. The bathroom included a shower. The main room had a large river stone fireplace in the southeast corner. Windows in every wall opened the cabin's interior to the surrounding forest where trees covered slopes rising toward white peaks often concealed by clouds.

"We're home Seth," shouted Clara. She entered the south bedroom and added, "If you agree, I'd like this room."

"A good choice," he confirmed before he started unloading more supplies. "We'll have to keep a fire going. When the fire is on we are home."

Stepping out of her new room, Clara said, "This cabin is right for us and we purchased some interesting supplies including bison or buffalo burgers. We can join all those people who, through the years dined on buffalo. People kept hunting when they should've stopped. Buffalo almost became extinct like so many other things. Our burgers come from ranches."

During our journey we've traveled further in discoveries than we have in miles. People miss the distance they could explore in revelations if the truth seen was just believed. So often people don't grow with the truth because it seems beyond believable.

Anyway, Sethrum, I've said enough about traveling. I'm going to make you the best bison burger ever seen in the west."

"Wonderful," he replied. "Could I help?"

"You could finish stocking the kitchen while I put to use what we've already unpacked," she replied.

"Teamwork is the best system," he said, before the kitchen became a busy place and soon, following aromas of cooking meat, the two travelers sat on chairs facing a fire snapping in the fireplace. They enjoyed a fist meal in the cabin.

"You were right about the burgers," he said. "They are the best."

"Yes they are," she agreed. "And so is this place. There's another area I can't seem to stop thinking about. You remember the clearing beside the river we passed today while driving here?"

"I do remember," he replied.

"Let's go back there tomorrow," she suggested. "Along with taking food, we might be able to catch a trout. If so, we could use Sara's method of cooking meat and spit the trout over a fire."

"I thought at the time the clearing was a place I would like to revisit," said Seth. "I'm pleased you feel the same way."

"This calls for an extra celebration," she declared, standing.

"Good idea," he said. "Meanwhile, I'll tidy up after your wonderful cooking."

A trace of wood smoke scented the room while the celebrants enjoyed wine and beer. The scene outside the windows gathered colors from the setting sun before darkening with the arrival of night. Through screens of partially open windows, the hooting of an owl sounded from the woods.

"I've always liked owls," said Seth, while Clara served another round. "The hooting of an owl marks the end of a perfect day."

"If it gets any more perfect, I'm going to need help finding my room," declared Clara.

"It's right where you left it," said Seth.

"That's the problem," countered Clara. "I hope I'll continue to remember where it is."

"You could sleep where you are," he suggested.

"Yes," she said. "And I think I'm going to. I look forward to seeing you in the morning with breakfast ready as you always have it prepared. Then we'll return to that place by the river and go fishing."

Seth awoke early as he always did. The moon dropped a patch of silver light on the cabin's floor near Clara who continued to sleep in her chair. Embers glowed in the fireplace. He looked out a side window just as a coyote walked through a pool of silver light beside the cabin.

After preparing coffee, Seth took some in a cup as he left the building and, in dawn's first glow, he walked along the same pathway used by the coyote. He followed the trail to a high, open area then sat down to sip the drink slowly, while watching first stirrings as dawn's light brightened.

There is likely, he mused, *no place unused by wildlife. I'm resting at the crossing of two trails. The path I used to get her continues to higher places. There's also a second trail cutting across the first. A crossing of trails provides a good location to watch and listen while actions of night close and those of the day begin.*

Westward, on the trail crossing the hillside, crows have started cawing. Crows are usually the first to add their calls to the start of a day. Those birds are always up to something.

The cawing has become a clamor and the ruckus is moving. Crows are following something and coming this way, noted Seth before he sipped more coffee, enjoying the forest as it changed to daytime life. *There's a coyote,* noted Seth *and it's coming this way. It's running at full speed along the trail and heading right at me. Soon this runner will be spilling my coffee.*

Thinking of having a coyote in his arms, Seth watched as the runner, about four feet away, saw him and stopped. The visitor then sat down, facing Seth.

Banff

Just as I've seen many dogs when they are having fun, thought Seth, *that coyote is playing and smiling.* After a few moments that seemed to be many more, the visitor stood up and walked a short distance back off the trail to greet a second, larger coyote.

The two have been racing, observed Seth. *They've been playing—enjoying their lives. This is a side of these beautiful animals people usually don't see. Wolves and coyotes have their own lives to live and they enjoy life. They have a role—and are part of the forest. They belong and are not just something to shoot or skin.*

The visitors walked past Seth and followed the trail down the slope. *The coyotes knew I was no threat to them*, thought Seth, *nor were they hostile to me. They seemed to accept a person having a morning coffee as a natural part of a day. Maybe I should get back. Clara will be awake.*

Following the trail back down the slope, Seth was surprised to see the coyotes again. They stayed ahead for a short distance before turning off the path and moving out of view.

Back at the cabin, Clara said, "Good morning. I've been making breakfast—flapjacks."

"Wonderful," he replied. "I've been out meeting some of the area's wildlife."

As he told her about the coyotes, breakfast preparations were completed. Plates topped by flapjacks were taken to chairs facing the fireplace where the travelers enjoyed this favorite way of starting a morning.

"Today," said Clara, "we could return to the clearing beside the river that seemed to welcome us. We could do some fishing, trying out some of our silver spoons."

"Good idea," he replied. "Maybe after we've fried up some bison burgers for lunch we could go."

"Yes," she said. "I prefer bison meat. It's leaner than beef."

After enjoying the first part of the day at the cabin, Clara and Seth drove to the clearing. "I like this place," declared Clara, having parked the car at the site. "I feel at home here—as if I've been at this location previously."

"I have the same response to this site," he added while they carried their equipment to the riverside. "I'll start a small fire we can enjoy while fishing."

Mergansers along with goldeneye and mallard ducks added their colors to the river's surface. Two loons called while flying past. A kingfisher hunted from an overhanging branch.

Seth and Clara sent silver spoons flashing out over the river to splash down and be drawn back. The sky turned colors from the setting sun when spray shot from the river's surface as a fish jumped upward, trying to throw a hook and line leading to Clara's fishing pole. A struggle continued until Seth helped bring to the bank a large rainbow trout.

"Maybe we could use the Sara Thomas technique of spitting this fish over the fire," suggested Clara. "That would be better than using our frying pan," agreed Seth. "I'll get the fish ready."

"Good," she declared. "I'll have everything else prepared."

The trout cooked over the fire had all the best of its flavor with the addition of a slight smoky seasoning. Topped by malt vinegar, salt and pepper, there resulted the finest fish dinners. "This wonderful meal," observed Seth, "helps to celebrate the enjoyment of being in this special place where we both can rest—savor a feeling of being at peace with life."

"Let's stay here for the night," suggested Clara.

"I'll get some boughs," replied Seth. "We could each make a mattress at the side of the fire. There are coats in the car to use as blankets."

Night settled onto the landscape, bringing silence broken only by the hooting of an owl. Wolves seemed to answer from distant slopes.

Darkness partially vanished with the advance of moonlight. It added a silvery sheen to the river's surface while sending shadows among trees.

"Time to get some sleep," suggested Seth before he looked away from the forest and saw Clara, as a spirit that might have just stepped out of the silver river. Clothed only in moonlight, she walked to Seth's side of the fire.

"This is only a visit," she said. "I like my own mattress."

"All visitors are welcome," he whispered.

"They'd better not all be welcome," she replied.

In the morning, they awoke on the same mattress and prepared for a new day. They drove to Chateau Lake Louise for breakfast. After enjoying much of the day in the region of turquoise lakes surrounded by mountains, the travelers returned to their cabin where they rekindled a fire in the fireplace. Following an evening snack, light outside the windows diminished as night arrived, announced by an owl.

"In the morning," said Clara, "at least once, I'd like to go with you when you leave for your walk in the first light of dawn."

"OK, great and I'll call you when coffee is ready," he answered.

"You have wonderful early morning walks, greeting each new day," she added, walking to her room.

"Mornings begin with sounds and sights not quite repeated at other times," he concluded.

"Be a good—new—experience for me," she added, before they slept.

"Coffee's ready," said Seth in what appeared to be darkness.

"Already?" asked Clara.

"A new day begins," he answered.

"Well, let's greet it," she said before getting up—slowly.

They left the cabin—each carrying a cup of coffee.

Seth led the way, following a different trail leading to high vistas. The climbers came to a clearing among trees where a view opened up to a landscape stretching through a cloak of mist to distant peaks.

"Should we stop before the drinks get cold?" asked Clara.

"Yes," he said. "The rocks ahead would provide a place to sit down."

Resting, sipping welcome warmth from cups, the travelers watched light add more distinct outlines to the region. Ravens called as the drinks were finished.

"Seth," said Clara. "Look along the path."

He turned in the direction she pointed and replied, "We are going to have company."

"Who would be around so early in the day?" she asked.

"We are about to find out," added Seth while the form came closer.

When the stranger's features could be seen, they were as craggy as rocky slopes although unthreatening.

"I have waited for you," said the man.

"Waited for us?" asked Clara.

"Yes," he replied. "I wanted to talk to you both at the same time and preferably at the start of a day when all things are new again and everything seems possible."

"Couldn't agree more," exclaimed Seth. "My favorite time of day."

"There's a place I would like to show you," offered the stranger, "although the walk is long."

Turning to Clara, Seth asked, "OK with you?"

"Let's not say no to what we haven't yet seen," she replied.

"We're ready," he told the man.

Without further comment the stranger started walking upward. As light increased, the path he followed became more visible. Ravens called often while the three climbers moved from one route to another into an adventure that held too much suspense to be tiring.

When traces of fatigue slowed their pace, Seth and Clara saw the man move among some bushes. He said, "We go in here."

Beyond shrubs, a short tunnel led to a chamber where the man lit a fire. It's light flickered along stone walls and across the surface of a sulfurous smelling pond.

"Sit down where you will be comfortable," directed the stranger. "I come to this hot spring often and you are welcome here any time."

"Thank you," said Seth. "Amazing that you would invite us here."

"You've been here before," countered the stranger. "Very few people know about this hot spring and there are others. The water is for healing."

"You say I've been here previously?" asked Seth.

"Yes," he confirmed. "You both have."

"You remember that clearing beside the river where you both slept last night?" he asked.

"I don't remember," said Seth. Clara looked at him and the three of them laughed.

"Well," continued the man, "that's where you both lived and intended to live longer many years ago when you, Seth James, were Charlie James and you, Clara Elder, were Barb Sims. Charlie built a log home there beside the river. He liked and felt drawn to the place where you both previously had lived when you were married and were Kootenay. That clearing is a traditional village site where fish were gathered and dried for the winter."

"How is all that possible?" asked Clara.

"We all have many lifetimes on earth—as many as we want to have," explained the man. "Some come here only once—others not at all. Many though might have fifty or more lives on earth. We come here to experience, develop and grow our spirits through hard knocks and adversity that do not exist on the other side—the spirit world—heaven where there is no trouble just continuous enjoyment and adventure of life—eternal life—of our spirits. You were here at the first years of Banff. As I have said, you were Charlie James and Barb Sims. You were going to get married but your plans were cut off when Charlie was shot and killed by three thieves, Reg, Len and Case. They stole Charlie's gold then used some of it to buy a secluded cabin from Howard Ridge. He moved into Banff and used some of the gold to rent a cabin from Barb while he built his new home. Barb then had proof of who had killed Charlie. She went to their secluded cabin and shot all three thieves, making the shooting look like the men had shot themselves during an argument. Barb worked for an outfitter, Isaac Thomas. They got married, had two children, a son and a daughter. You met one of your descendants when you took that trail ride with Sara Thomas."

Stopping, the stranger added kindling to the flame. Additional light danced across rock walls, revealing a carving of a great bear.

"This is all so fantastic," gasped Clara. Looking at Seth, she whispered, "Are we dreaming?"

"This is no dream," explained the man. Although he spoke softly, his voice filled the cave and seemed to be coming from all directions, including the past and the future. "All of life is amazing—in its ultimate perfection although occasionally the process might seem to be brutal, but the evil is only done by people who have turned away from the Creator who would never turn away from people. Individuals make their own hell. The Creator—all kindness—would not do this harm to us. By the way, there is both Father God and Mother God. Why do you think everything on earth is distributed male and female?" The words stopped while flames moved and light danced.

"When you were here as Charlie James and Barb Sims," continued the voice, "you both—although you didn't fully talk about such intentions—wanted to get married and have life together. The shooting of Charlie blocked your plans. You both wanted another chance. You are back and this is your second chance."

After stopping, the softy spoken yet easily heard words, sounding ageless, started again when the stranger said, "I have a request. I would like you to visit a restaurant in Banff. The owner is a woman called Sally Gray Hawk. She is a chef and owner but is currently attending university. She is planning to end her classes and concentrate on the restaurant business. My request is for you to visit her and tell her she should continue taking courses to be a lawyer. This will enable her to help maintain the traditions with language and culture. She will work to have the treaties recognized and updated—like all long-standing agreements—not to take anything from others but for the Indigenous people to have their rightful place as a founding culture of the Americas—of Canada and the United States."

"It is a pleasure—an honor—to take your message," whispered Clara. "I'm curious, however, about why you wouldn't stay by her side and deliver your message yourself?"

"If we stay beside people and help them so they have no mistakes—no trouble—no choices to make then there would be no reason for them to come to earth for a life here," answered the man. "The learning and development comes from facing obstacles and making choices. We appear sometimes as a stranger, as a hunch, as a feeling in the morning of the way to turn and occasionally we add a nudge to keep each person traveling in the right direction without a useless waste of time. You shouldn't waste your time. It is precious and an opportunity."

"You are kind to give us such a helpful nudge to deliver," said Seth, "and thank you for telling us about us. We have a second chance?"

"That's right," he answered, "and you have choices to make. That's why you are here."

"Maybe it's about time you asked me to marry you," stated Clara, encouraged to talk by all she had heard.

"I wanted to wait until I was sure I wouldn't get rejected," he replied.

"If you wait any longer you'll get more than a rejection," she stated, before they all laughed.

"Well Seth?" asked the stranger.

"Clara or Barb," said Seth, "would you marry me?"

"I have to think about it," she said and the men both were shocked before she said, "Yes" and they all laughed.

"Some things take a long time," said the man.

"Lifetimes even," added Clara.

"Stranger," said Seth to the man. "This is the first time I've known anyone who I knew was a friend before I even knew the person's name."

In his unhurried way the man replied, "Sally was at one time my granddaughter although our family descriptions changed as years go by on earth. We don't mark time in the spirit world where there is no distinction between past, present and future. All is one. When Sally was my granddaughter, her name was Raven. My name is Gray Hawk."

Chapter 11

Going Back

After again enjoying an extraordinary breakfast at Chateau Lake Louise, Seth and Clara returned for another trail ride at the Thomas Ranch. Their car stopped at the ranch's parking lot just as Sara Thomas and the other riders were ready to leave.

"Just in time," said Sara in greeting. "Your horses are ready." The line of riders left the ranch, following a trail that was new only to the customers.

"Sort of like being a rider on a bus," said Clara to Seth who was directly behind her.

"Yes," agreed Seth. "The driver and horses are accustomed to the route."

"Would be interesting to know the horse we are riding," continued Clara. "Such a connection would add a grander dimension to the journey."

"We've missed that extra bond with the horses but you've gained it with Sara," observed Seth.

"Yes," exclaimed Clara. "I'll be mentioning our connection to her. According to the weather, we are part of a perfect day. Clouds are drifting slowly overhead where an eagle is resting on air currents. Sunlight is emblazing distant peaks. Forests are like green carpets sloping down into the valley."

"There's a large river in the valley," noted Seth. "Must be the Bow."

When the riders dismounted at the trail ride's destination, there were two women fishing from a bank of the Bow River. Both women were lean and seemed to be strong.

"Hope you don't mind company," said Sara to the two women."

"We always meet other people when we fish here," replied one of them. She had lines of friendliness around her dark eyes. A deep tan darkened her face where a strong jaw indicated part of her personality. Her hair was black although graying. "We usually meet people so we bring extra supplies. They are now staying cold in the river." Her eyes sparkled with an apparently adventurous spirit as she said, "I'm Rose Carlson and my friend is Cathy Sloan." The other woman had long blondish hair gathered in braids at the back of her head, adding some decoration to otherwise plain features.

"You are welcome to join us for a meal," said Sara.

"Thank you," replied Rose. "We can add a rainbow trout to the food."

"We could spit it over the fire," added Sara. "We'll be cooking beef steaks the same way."

"Another fine day at the Bow River fishing place," observed Cathy. "We usually meet fishermen here—or tourists. You are our first riders."

"The horses will want to drink from the river and graze," said Sara to the riders. "I'll start the fire and set up some skewers. We'll be having beefsteaks and rainbow trout cooked over flames along with baked potatoes. The meal will be served on paper plates."

After enjoying delicious and tender food, the riders rested on the riverbank, while the water swirled past adding to calmness of the day. "You've shared your supplies," said Rose before she stepped into the water. "Time for us to share what we brought for ourselves along with people we meet." She reached into the water and, helped by Cathy, withdrew bottles of wine and cans of beer.

"The river provides," announced Cathy after tea and coffee were finished and cups were refilled with wine. A few people, including Seth, selected beer.

"Life is full of surprises," he exclaimed after receiving two chilled cans of beer. "You ladies are topping off a perfect day." Turning to Clara, he added, "The scenery of the Bow Valley is beyond the highest expectations—like the people we meet."

"We came on a holiday," replied Clara. "We didn't realize when we started out we would not only travel along roads but through our lives and the journey is the length of many generations."

Sara refilled cups and brought more beer to Seth. To her, Clara said, "Please sit down for a few minutes."

With Sara sipping wine and relaxing on one side and Seth enjoying beer on the other, Clara turned to Sara and said, "Early this morning, we discovered that you and I are related—quite closely—but the story is so fantastic you might not believe it."

"And I thought two women serving beer and wine was a big surprise," exclaimed Sara. "I suppose next I'll hear I'm related to my horse."

When the three stopped laughing, Clara continued, "As I said, you might not believe me but this morning Seth and I met a stranger—a spirit—and he said that this happens more often than we are aware. We might get a hunch, a nudge to do something, hear a voice, awaken with an idea or, like this morning—meet a stranger. He said his name was Gray Hawk, an ancestor of Sally Gray Hawk who owns a restaurant in Banff. We are going to visit her after this trail ride."

"I know Sally," said Sara. "She is a friend. She comes here for rides and we enjoy her restaurant."

"The stranger we met on our walk, Gray Hawk, is a spiritual person from the other side, the spiritual world—heaven. He said life is immortal and we come to earth maybe many times to learn and develop. In an earlier lifetime here on earth he said I was Barb Sims. She was going to marry Charlie James but three thieves killed him. Barb later married Isaac Thomas and they had two children, a son and a daughter. They started this ranch. Thereby you and I are directly related. He also said Seth was Charlie James."

"Wow," gasped Sara. "That's a lot of surprises to get at once—a lot to think about. I'll talk to Sally about Gray Hawk. When we get back to the ranch, I'll show you some pictures."

Standing up and smiling, Sara asked, "Have I had too much wine or did you actually tell me what I just heard?"

"You heard correctly," she answered. "Life shows us a lot of information. Being aware of it—and believing what we encounter is a choice we have to make and our reaction determines our lives."

During the ride back to the ranch, Seth said to Clara, "You sent out the words. I wonder how they are being received."

"Might take some time to know and we won't be here very long," she replied. "I like Sara."

At the ranch, the horses were cared for while riders returned to their vehicles and started driving out the lane. After a slight film of dust settled, Sara approached Clara and Seth then said, "Thank you for staying as I requested. There are some pictures you might want to see. Please come inside the house."

Logs of the structure's interior had darkened through time. Rooms were large and spacious, containing paintings of the west. Sara brought her guests to see one wall in particular. It was covered with photographs depicting the ranch's and Banff's beginnings along with current prints.

Some photographs held the visitors' attention longer than others until one framed print stopped both Seth and Clara. They looked no further. They stared at the two people named Barb Sims and Charlie James.

"When convenient sometime during a visit for another trail ride, could we get a copy of this picture?" asked Clara.

"I'll have that ready for you," Sara answered. "When I look at this picture on the wall, I'll never see it the same way again and I'll talk to Sally about Gray Hawk."

Chapter 12

The Message

After leaving the ranch, Seth said, "Have we had enough for one day or should we go to the restaurant?"

"We should take care of our responsibilities then we can rest," said Clara.

"I saw it that way and I'm glad you agree," he said, while Clara continued driving. They drove the rest of the way with each one having much to think about and not ready to sort out their lives by searching through conversation.

Clara and Seth parked their car on a lot next to a sprawling log building that was a match for surrounding forested slopes of the mountains. The restaurant's interior contained frontier elegance representative of wilderness landscapes along with legendary people. Clearly this was not a recently built structure but one from the history of Banff.

A lady who accompanied them to a table wore a blue blouse topping a black dress with leather belt containing a silver buckle. Bracelets clinked from her wrists as she dropped menus in front of her two guests. Long black hair bordered her attractive face where dark brown eyes sparkled when she asked, "Anything from the bar?"

"House wine, please," replied Clara.

"And draft," added Seth.

"We're not very busy this time of day," noted the woman. "Most people arrive in the evening. "I'm Sophie."

She walked away, returning quickly with the drinks. "Ready to order," she asked.

"Arctic char with home fries," answered Clara.

"The same please," added Seth.

Sophie left, leaving Seth and Clara time to sip drinks while enjoying grandeur of surrounding scenery. "How can we begin to even think about all that has happened?" asked Seth.

"Evening with a fire in the fireplace at our cabin will give us the rest and opportunity to slowly unfold the information we've gathered," submitted Clara.

"Those are the moments in life I savor," he said.

"I look forward to them also," Clara said. "For now though, a great meal is arriving."

"David Thompson and his family, along with other adventurers dined on much the same foods as we've enjoyed," observed Seth after savoring a meal of the finest fish and special home fries. "But those early travelers didn't get the service we've experienced. While Thompson mapped western Canada, Lewis and Clark were visiting the western United States. These travelers mapped routes used for thousands of years by Indigenous people. So using the word discovery is as incorrect as much of what is written in our history books. History is as accurate today as any person's opinion. An unexamined story is one that will be misunderstood. The same could be said of a ballad or other legend presenting history. We have some amazing history to relate to Sally Gray Hawk.

Sophie approached and asked, "Will there be anything else?"

"Yes," answered Clara. "We would like to talk to Sally Gray Hawk."

"Sally is owner and chef," replied Sophie. "She usually doesn't have time to meet guests."

"We are messengers," continued Clara.

"And your message is?" asked Sophie.

"From Gray Hawk," replied Clara.

Sophie walked away, giving Clara and Seth further time to enjoy the elegance of the building along with magnificence of outside scenery.

"An interesting end to a day—that has seen a journey through our lives," observed Seth.

"Yes," agreed Clara, "and the ride continues."

A strikingly attractive woman approached their table. Long, black hair was swept away and tied behind a narrow face of finely etched features surrounding black eyes where fire burned.

"Will this take long?" she asked. "I'm Sally Gray Hawk."

"Please sit down," suggested Clara before the woman sat, relaxed and explained, "Sophie said you are messengers."

"Yes," noted Clara. "This morning when we went for an early, break of dawn walk, we met a stranger who took us to a cave with a hot spring. By the light of a small fire, he told us a story. He said his name was Gray Hawk. He always visits the cave and has been coming there since earliest days when you were his granddaughter. He has remained to watch you through your lives. Occasionally he sends you a message. They arrive in different forms, appearing as a hunch, a nudge, a voice or, in this case, a visit from messengers. He said you have been wondering if you should continue with university. He said you should become a lawyer to help keep the traditional language and culture. Also you could work to have the treaties recognized, respected and updated, not to take from others but for the Indigenous people to have their rightful place as a founding culture of Canada."

Sally's face brightened and she whispered, "That advice couldn't come at a better time. He must've known. Now I know where I'm going."

"You work with tourists who visit Banff," said Seth. "What do you think is the most important message Banff has to offer?"

Fire showed in Sally's eyes when she replied, "There's grandeur in the buildings and the accomplishments of constructing them. There is vision in establishing the railway. For thousands of years the Indigenous people kept this area in its original state to the extent that those who came later said they discovered each place as though no other people had been here first. Most important though is the message of the mountains themselves and wilderness for in their spirit there is the Creator."

Turning to Seth, Clara said, "At the beginning of this journey I told you I was looking for a story. Now I have my story."

About the Author

Daniel Hance Page is a freelance writer with twenty-seven books published and others being written. His books are authentic stories filled with action, adventure, history and travel, including Native American traditions and spiritual insights to protect our environment in the smallest park or widest wilderness.

Made in the USA
Monee, IL
30 May 2021